TIMENELL

By

Stephen Martin Fritz

Illustrated by Julian Fritz
Edited by Denise Morel and Kristina Fritz

Table of Contents

Chapter 1

Prelude

Date: Friday, September 5, 2042

Location: International Space Exploration Training Center, central Georgia, USA

In 2020, Anna Schmitt was recruited from Germany's National Academy of Science to head up the Computational Astrophysics division at NASA. Ten years later, her leadership and job proficiency earned her a promotion to Chief Scientist of NASA'S Development Directorate, in charge of the most important mission ever undertaken by man.

As Chief Scientist, she had to temper the pleasure that comes with working alongside the most brilliant scientists in the world with the tedium of having to oversee, review, and approve every report produced in the directory. She was also the final authority on personnel decisions. Sometimes those decisions came with joy, and sometimes they came with disappointment.

There was a soft knock on her office door. Knowing that it was Wayne Sharon, she beckoned him in.

A tall, confident, and good-looking man strode up to her desk. Dr. Schmitt pointed to a chair, inviting him to sit down.

Wayne is a highly trained agronomics specialist. He carries himself well, is always assertive, and even dominant at times. He was confident that he was being called into the lead scientist's office to be congratulated for having been accepted as the final crew member for the sixteen-year top-secret NASA space mission he had trained so very hard for. In fact, he was hoping to be named leader of the mission.

"Mr. Sharon," Dr. Schmitt began, "as you know, the final composition of our crew was determined this week.The last position to be filled was the crew's agronomist.The two final contenders for that position were you and Mr. Sutton. I am sorry to have to inform you that the committee of scientists and psychologists in charge of that decision has chosen Mr. Sutton as the last member of the crew."

Wayne was dumbfounded. He stared for a few seconds at the giant NASA logo on the rug in front of Dr. Schmitt's desk, before he finally spoke up."You mean that screwball, Willie

Sutton, has been chosen over me! I can't believe it. It never crossed my mind that it would be me who was eliminated."

"I know this must be quite a disappointment," the doctor acknowledged in a sympathetic tone, "but when … "

"I've never washed-out of anything," Wayne interrupted.

Dr. Schmitt continued in a steady voice. "Today is Friday. When you come into work on Monday, please report to the mission center for procurement. You're being reassigned to the group loading final provisions for the crew. It is quite an important position, where no mistakes can be tolerated. Your professionalism is needed there. In fact, you'll be briefed on the full details of the mission even before the crew members are."

"Huh?" Wayne looked up, confused and visibly unhappy. "That's small consolation Dr. Schmitt. I'm going from possibly being a team member on the most important mission in history to a glorified stock-boy! And you expect me to be proud of that?"

The doctor paused for a moment, shuffling some papers on her desk and hoping Wayne would regain his composure.

"I expect you to do your job, Mr. Sharon, as we all must do ours. Don't you think every one of us here has wished, at one time or another, to be going on this mission?" she responded empathetically.

"At one time or another maybe," Wayne interjected. "But this sort of mission is all I have lived for, all I have thought about, and even all I have dreamed about, for my entire life. When I was selected for consideration more than two years ago,

I threw myself into this effort. This is unreasonable. Who made this decision? Can I see the report that shows why Sutton was chosen over me? It has to be wrong!"

The doctor shook her head and responded, "Your technical and behavioral evaluations will be sent to your desk a few days after the crew's departure."

Clearly shaken, Wayne responded rhetorically, "I just can't believe this! This has to be a mistake. Can I go now?"

Not waiting for a response, he got out of his chair and strode with frustrated determination out of the room.

Chapter 2

The Briefing

Wednesday, September 10, 2042

Location: International Space Exploration Training Center, central Georgia, USA

The secluded cafeteria within the top-secret military training facility buzzed with anticipation as Liz and Willie waited for their final briefing. They had been chosen from dozens of highly capable candidates to be part of something historic. Liz could feel her heart pounding in her chest, and she was sure Willie could hear it, too.

As they sat across from each other, they couldn't help but let their minds wander to what could lie ahead.

Liz felt both excited and nervous. Their two-year training program, that began with 24 prospective participants had painstakingly been whittled down to the final eight crew members. Their long training and grueling competition was finally over, and today they would be finding out the details of the space mission they had volunteered for.

"I can't believe it's finally happening!" she said to Willie, fidgeting with excitement.

"Relax, Liz. Remember, in space, you won't have to worry about your hair getting messed up," Willie teased, trying to create a more relaxed atmosphere.

Liz gave him a playful punch on his arm. "You're a real comfort, you know that?" she said with a grin.

"Trust me, Liz, I totally get where you're coming from," Willie shared understandingly. "It's been a long two years of training, and I'm ready to get on with it. If I hadn't met you, I might have withdrawn from this project or even been happy to be kicked off the team."

"Kicked off of our team? What do you mean?" Liz inquired; her curiosity piqued.

"I got into an argument with that guy Nicholas Popov the other day. I had seen the two of you talking in the hall, and it sure looked like he was coming on to you," Willie said with an accusing glare.

Liz was somewhat dismayed by Willie's apparent jealousy. Having volunteered to participate in a 16-year space mission, she had given up the idea of marriage and a family, and by extension, any serious romantic relationship that could jeopardize her resolve.

Not wishing to hurt his feelings, she set aside her apprehension and playfully rolled her eyes. "Oh, Willie, you've got quite the imagination," she teased. "You think everyone has a thing for me. But come on – were you two really arguing about me?"

Willie tilted his head to the side and grinned. "Nah, it's not that," he lied. "I just don't like his attitude. It's just his whole 'Mr. Know-It-All' act that gets under my skin, you know?"

"Well, he is supposed to know everything about physical fitness," Liz said, trying to reason with Willie. "That's his area of expertise. Every one of our crew members is an expert in their field. You're just a bit of a hot head."

Suddenly, she noticed that other members were rising from their chairs. She turned toward the cafeteria entrance and said, "Look, they're signaling for us to go into the conference room."

The two got up from their seats and started making their way toward the briefing area.

"You're probably right," Willie admitted, giving a thoughtful nod. "I actually apologized to him. Besides, I can't afford to be thrown off the team now. I was almost beaten out for this position by that guy, Wayne Sharon. You know him: he was in the survivalist class we were all made to take. It came down to the two of us being selected as the final member of the crew."

Willie let out a deep breath as he continued, "I've put too much time and effort into my training and when we get back, we're going to have big paychecks waiting for us. I don't want to miss out on that. Plus, I don't want you going anywhere for 16 years without me."

She grinned and concurred, "We can't spend our salaries out in space. And 16 years of back pay should amount to a fortune. What's the first thing you're going to do with your money when we return to Earth?" she asked.

"Buy you dinner, of course," he grinned, already knowing the answer.

As they both shared a laugh, the pressure that had been weighing on them seemed to melt away, if only for a moment.

"They say we'll be welcomed back as heroes. I guess the public will be made aware of our trip sometime after we're gone. No one knows about it now," Liz continued, as her nerves began to tingle again. "This is our final briefing, and tomorrow, we're off."

Willie placed a reassuring hand on her shoulder and gave her a warm smile. "Don't worry, Liz, we're the best of the best, and we'll make it back home safely. And when we do, we'll be, if not the richest people on Earth, undoubtedly the most famous," he said.

Liz nodded in agreement. She knew that they were in for the adventure of a lifetime. "Alright, let's buckle up! Time to dive into the extraordinary!" she said enthusiastically.

The tension was palpable as the final eight-person team filed into the briefing room and took their seats. All eyes were on the podium where the briefer, the Russian Captain Debra Ivanov, stood poised and ready to deliver what would undoubtedly be the most important information of their lives.

With a noticeable Russian accent and a steady voice, Captain Ivanov began, "You have been assembled here for your last briefing."

The team held its collective breath as the captain continued, "This cadre began with twenty four volunteers, and it has been whittled down to its final eight participants. You have been strategically selected for your specialized skills and adaptability. You have volunteered for an internationally manned, 16-year, inter-stellar space mission, a journey that will take you farther than any human has ever gone before."

Silence filled the room, the weight of the situation settling on everyone.

"Each of you has been selected not only for your skills but also because you are single with no dependents. You have undergone psychological evaluations for adaptability, stability, and cooperative tendencies. Your group has been in training for two years, and each of you has understandably expressed a desire to move on to the mission itself.

“That day has arrived.

“You have been informed that yours would be the most historic space flight in human history. It would be a 16-year mission to explore beyond the solar system. You have been instructed to speak to no one but each other about the nature of this mission. After you are gone, the details of your trip will be made known to the world, and it is quite likely that you will become celebrities."

Suspense filled the air as Captain Ivanov paused for effect. "Today marks the day you'll learn all the details of that mission. Sit back, because what you are about to hear is the most fantastic story in human history, and the success or failure of your mission may determine the future of mankind itself."

Liz smirked, imagining the captain was being a little melodramatic.

"Allow me to start from the very beginning," Captain Ivanov began, "As you all know, in 1942, the government of the United States launched the Manhattan Project with the aim of developing atomic power. From this project came the atomic bombs used over Hiroshima and Nagasaki in 1945.

"What you do not know is that the creation of bombs was not the real mission of the Manhattan Project. The bombs were just a bonus, a side-effect of what the physicists were really after.

"The primary purpose of the Manhattan Project was to develop atomic energy, and this energy was intended for a purpose far more important than creating bombs.

"Albert Einstein's revolutionary equation, '$E=mc^2$,' and his theory of relativity transformed our understanding of energy and matter, demonstrating that they were interchangeable. In the 1920s, Werner Heisenberg's Quantum Mechanics added to this, implying that not only were matter and energy interchangeable but that time and space might be interchangeable as well.

"By merging these radical concepts, the world's top scientists recognized that not only were the secrets to nearly infinite power within humanity's reach but also the ability to convert current time into future time and back again.

"In short, what the scientists discovered was that the same enormous power that could blast away matter could be used to blast away time. They hypothesized the existence of something called "Quantum Time" and realized that with enough power, such as that provided by atomic energy, traveling through time was indeed a real possibility.

"There have been many travelers through space, but tomorrow, the eight of you will become mankind's first travelers through time!"

As soon as the announcement was made, the eight trainees looked at each other and began to squirm in their seats.

"From this point forward, this mission will be referred to as **'Timenell.'** The name of this mission, like everything else about it, is beyond Top Secret. You will not repeat this name outside of this facility or to anyone but yourselves and our team.

"The possibility of time travel has been revealed through certain equations by theoretical physicists. It involves numerous technical details that are unimportant to you. All you need to know is that it works and has been proven to work on several occasions in the past. I've been asked to brief you on the developments in time travel from the 1940s until today.

"What makes time travel possible is enormous energy.

Atomic power was first harnessed for time travel in 1946. Theoretical physicists told us that traveling through time was possible, but their equations indicated that it could only occur in quantum-time increments of approximately 9,100 years.

"The construction of the fabric of the universe itself allows for time travel, but it prevents us from going back and seeing our grandparents as babies or witnessing our own high school graduations. It is possible to travel through time, but it must be in roughly 9,100-year increments. We can send someone or something 9,100 years into the future or 9,100 years into the past.

"Or we could double it and send them 18,200 years into the future or 18,200 years into the past. Or 27,300 years forwards or back, etc., always in increments of 9,100 years.

"Furthermore, there are small windows in which these trips must begin and end. The scientists tell us that we cannot send someone through time any day we please. The researchers also inform us that we are very restricted in another way. There is a window of approximately 182,000 seconds, that is, about 2 days, where we can send someone through time. If we miss that opportunity, we have to wait 16 years for it to come around again.

"The farther one travels, the more energy is required. It takes a huge amount of energy to send something 9,100 years into the past or future. It takes 100 thousand times that amount to send them 18,200 years, and 100 million times that amount to send them 27,300 years out. So clearly, only the shortest amount of time travel is feasible for us today.

"When it was first realized that atomic power allowed us to send something back or forward in time, the limited amount of atomic power available to us in 1946 made only the shortest trip possible—a journey of 9,100 years—and allowed for only about 400 kilograms, or about 880 pounds, to travel across time.

"Luckily, all this power is only necessary to send something forward or backward in time. Absolutely no power at all is required to bring it back to our time. In fact, whatever is sent comes back on its own, and it cannot be prevented from coming back.

“One intriguing feature of quantum time was that whatever was sent back or forth in time would automatically return back to us 16 years and 22 days later. For some reason, this aspect represented another unique facet of quantum time. Anything sent either forward or backward in time would remain in the future or the past for 16 years and 22 days, and then suddenly, it would be returned to the time period from which it originated.

"However, it would not return to the date it was sent. For both the travelers and the people remaining back home, 16 years and 22 days would pass. So, for both the travelers and the individuals staying behind, anything we send forward today will be returned 16 years and 22 days later and everyone, both there and here, would be 16 years and 22 days older."

As Captain Ivanov paused for a moment, a couple of hands in the audience shot up in anticipation.

"Please save your questions until after I've concluded the briefing. I have a lot of information to share with you."

Captain Ivanov then proceeded to offer a meticulous narrative detailing the sequence of events that led to the creation of the groundbreaking technology.

"The scientists and military personnel of 1945 collaborated to create a briefing paper to be presented to Franklin Roosevelt, the President of the United States at the time. The President was informed that a video and audio recording device could be developed weighing under 880 pounds. This device would have the capability to be sent into either the future or the past, where it would remain for the 16-year period, capturing short bursts of video and audio recordings, along with measurements of temperature and daylight.

"It could have been made ready to go by 1946, and upon its return in 1962, the data could be viewed and analyzed.

"However, there was only enough power for a single trip, either forward or backward in time. It would be up to the president to decide in which direction our instruments were to be sent."

In the room, behind Captain Ivanov, stood a large screen displaying an image of Franklin Roosevelt being briefed by scientists.

She continued, "The atmosphere at the White House was intense as two opposing arguments were presented, each with their own merits.

"The first group of scientists advocated for sending a camera system back in time 9,100 years. They believed that by traveling back in time, we might capture images of how our early ancestors developed. Pictures of the first cities and recordings of the earliest languages could be made. All might be captured and brought back to us. This would significantly enhance our understanding of human history and anthropology, uncovering mysteries and unlocking secrets that have long been hidden.

"When they were done speaking, the second group of scientists and military leaders stepped forward, advocating for a journey into the future. They suggested that such a trip could offer a glimpse into new wonder weapons and technological advancements that are as yet unimaginable. Additionally, it could also provide us with insights into cures for currently untreatable diseases and other medical breakthroughs that would revolutionize our way of life.

"This last suggestion caught the President's attention.

"Being bound to a wheelchair by polio, an incurable disease at the time, the prospect of a cure being brought back from the future piqued his interest. He then inquired whether it might be possible to send machines in both directions. He was informed that the energy required for two trips was simply not available and that the cost of each trip was roughly equivalent to the annual cost of the entire World War. It was made clear that not even America, the richest nation on Earth, could afford such an endeavor.

"Roosevelt thought for less than a minute before declaring that it was our duty to look to the future. He asserted that the probe and all its equipment must be sent forward 9100 years to discover everything that could be learned from tomorrow and to bring it back for our profitable exploitation today.

"So, as the year 1945 drew to a close, construction of the probe began. An audiovisual system was created, and on April 25th, 1946, within that two-day window that occurs once every 16 years, power was applied, and the audiovisual recording machine disappeared. Those who were present said that it was like a magician's act whoosh! It vanished right in front of them!

"Then, the team of time-scientists disassembled back to their universities and laboratories.

"World War II ended, and the Cold War began. Sixteen years and twenty-two days later, the team was reassembled at the very spot from where the time probe had been sent. By this time, many of the original team members had retired, and many of those who were assembled speculated that the 880-pound device would not actually return. Instead, they suggested that with all that power, the machine had merely been vaporized. Everyone stood around and looked at their watches.

"Miraculously, and just as the theory predicted, the audiovisual machine suddenly reappeared.

"Had it truly returned from 9100 years into the future?

"Anxiously, the scientists and military personnel disassembled it and painstakingly watched and listened to hours and hours of recordings. Everything seemed to have gone perfectly.

"However, there was one disconcerting observation.

"The recording had turned on and off for a few minutes every few days for 16 years. It captured everything from blue skies and clouds to full moons and sunsets. It recorded birds flying, rabbits bounding, and bees buzzing. Everything appeared as expected. The only puzzling aspect was that not once in 16 years and 22 days did the camera capture a single sign of human life no planes going overhead, no stray hiker passing by, no buildings, nothing.

"The group of scientists were perplexed and didn't know what to make of this.

"At the 1962 quantum time cycle, another recording machine had been prepared to go. A day later, it was sent. This time, it was an even larger and more sophisticated device. Sixteen years later, in 1978, it too returned, but interestingly, not in exactly the same spot.

"It materialized, dented, and scratched, about 15 feet from the spot where it had been sent. Apparently, a black bear had stumbled onto it and bounced it around a bit. A picture of the creature's nose was recorded as a close-up on the film. It was determined that wherever the device was moved to while in the future, that would be the same spot it would return to, when it came back to us here in the past.

"If somehow it had been moved a mile away in the future, upon its return, it would reappear in that spot, a mile away from us.

"By the 1970s, scientists from Soviet Russia and communist China had also deciphered the implications of the physicists' equations, and both nations figured out what America was up to in time travel.

"In response to this, American President Richard Nixon, under the guise of détente and in an effort to improve Cold War relations, visited both Moscow and Beijing to propose a joint venture in time travel. Of course, the true nature of these meetings was kept secret from the public.

"As the planning for the mission progressed, it became evident that the devices the scientists intended to send had grown to enormous proportions, and the costs of the mission had surged as well. To address this challenge, it was decided to let all the nuclear powers in on the secret, and seek their assistance in developing and financing future missions. The nations of France, Great Britain, India, and Pakistan became involved.

"By the 1978 quantum time phase, all nuclear capable nations were participating, and a larger, more elaborate probe was sent. When that probe returned in 1994, it too showed no human activity. At this juncture, the participants concluded that there must be something wrong with the location from where the probe was being launched.

"The devices had all been launched from a location in central Colorado. Maybe, for some unknown reason, this area simply did not appeal to future humans. Or maybe future technological changes allowed all of humanity to live in tight cities, leaving vast swaths of countryside open and uninhabited.

"Of course, there was no time to change the location of the fourth mission, which departed in 1994 and returned in 2010, still with no signs of human activity. During that interval, it was decided that two smaller probes would be sent in the 2010 phase and that they would be launched from two distinct locations. One was set up and sent forward by the Russians from a location near the Volga River. The probe being sent forward by the Americans was moved to its present site, a location not far from where we are today, in central Georgia.

"Both came back intact, but still with no trace of human activity identified.

"The most recent probes were sent in 2026; they were by far the largest and most sophisticated devices sent forward to date. The American probe was equipped with a wide range of advanced instruments that measured various atmospheric and environmental factors, such as oxygen and nitrogen levels, radioactivity, carbon dioxide content, and even soil microorganisms. Additionally, it emitted strange sounds to attract passersby for photographing, making it quite an interesting device.

"On the other hand, the Russian time probe was designed to test the effects of time travel on living organisms. It carried a hardy, small, tough, slow-growing shrub. This plant could be expected to live and last for the 16 years it was to exist in the future. It could be examined upon its return to ensure that living things could pass back and forth through time without suffering any ill effects.

"This morning, both the Russian and American systems returned safely to Earth, and all recorded data showed normal levels of elements, compounds, and radiation factors similar to those found on our planet today. The plant sent by the Russians returned alive and healthy. It was quickly dissected and examined in microscopic detail, showing no apparent signs of stress. It has grown as anticipated and appears perfectly normal in every way. The Russian and American systems that had been sent during the last phase weighed 18 tons each. They recorded almost continuously for 16 years.

"But again, in our superficial examination of the probes, it appears that neither the Russian nor the American devices detected any sign of human life. Not a trace.

"And by now, you have undoubtedly figured out why you are here. With that said, I will turn you over to the commander of this mission, General Yadev."

Chapter 3
The Mission

General Yadev, the man in charge of India's space program, stepped up to the podium. "Good morning, crew," he exclaimed in a firm voice, speaking English but with a heavy Indian accent. "I place my utmost trust in each of you, confident that you have fully grasped the unique and crucial nature of the mission you are about to embark upon. Your job is to uncover the mystery of humanity's destiny. We need to know whether or not humans still exist in the future.

"To achieve this, you will travel ahead in time 9,100 years and find out what is going on.

"Have humans moved underground? Have we gone extinct? Did we kill each other off in nuclear wars? Or are the humans of tomorrow simply living in areas not yet investigated by our probes? It is up to you, eight brave time travelers, to discover what has happened to humanity.

"The participating nations have once again combined their resources, this time to send forward one giant compound, far larger than anything tried before, to serve as your living and working quarters while you explore the world of the future. A full inventory of your provisions will be available to you upon your departure in the morning. Your equipment includes 24 long-range drones, four small all-terrain electric vehicles, stethoscopes, extra pairs of boots, toothbrushes, terrain maps, and everything else our team of experts could anticipate that you might need within the weight limits of our capabilities.

"It is predicted that moving an enormous amount of material over time will require an unprecedented amount of energy. For this reason, in recent years, America and other nuclear powers have begun rebuilding nuclear generating stations. Once you are time phased forward, the amount of power drawn from Earth-bound systems will be so significant that it will cause a temporary blackout along the East Coast of the United States.

"This event is expected to cause a stir and make headlines in the news media. However, in an effort to forestall any unwanted curiosity, press releases to multiple news organizations have already been drafted to announce that the blackout was caused by a faulty wiring system in the American power grid. Additionally, other stories are set to be planted in the news media, such as suggestions that it may be terrorist computer hackers trying to get hold of the world's electrical systems or other forms of sabotage. Every effort will be made to send the curious away from the real facts of the situation.

"We have struggled to keep this information away from the general public so as not to cause alarm. However, with so many nations now participating, it cannot be kept secret for long. And with your very lives on the line, it wouldn't be right to do so.

"Therefore, shortly after your departure, the world will be informed of the details of your mission. Everyone will be reassured that if humanity has run into some sort of trouble, your team will find out about it and return with the information, thereby allowing us to avoid any catastrophe."

The General paused for a few seconds, allowing the team members to absorb what they had just been told before introducing the next speaker, Dr. Schmitt, from Germany. She is the lead scientist in charge of all preparations for the mission.

“Doctor Schmitt will not be able to stay very long," he explained, "as she has to oversee all last-minute preparations for your send-off."

Doctor Schmitt, in her native German accent, stepped to the podium:

"I wish you all good luck. There is nothing to worry about. We have anticipated your every need and trained you to handle every contingency. You will arrive safely in the future and return 16 years from now. We are confident of that.

"What we don't know is what has happened to humanity. I hope, for all our sakes, that you can find out.

"Please excuse me; I have some last-minute details to attend to. General Yadev will now return to the podium to answer any questions."

Eight hands shot up simultaneously.

General Yadev continued, "As you have been told, **Timenell** is the most expensive, most highly classified, and most important mission in the history of mankind. Before I take any questions, I'd like to brief you on the biographical details of the companions who will be accompanying you for the next 16 years of your lives.

“From now on, you are a team, a highly trained and supremely intelligent team by the way. I have been told that the average IQ of this group is over 135. It is right that you know who your fellow teammates are. I will answer your questions after Captain Ivanov completes her portion of your briefing. She will inform you of the origins, education, and qualifications of each of your fellow travelers." He stepped aside to allow the captain to replace him at the podium.

Captain Ivanov reclaimed the podium, "Thank you, sir. While all of you have crossed paths before and some of you have trained together, it's imperative for each of you to be familiar with the skills and responsibilities of the other members of your team. Your collaboration will be integral to the success of this mission."

Her words were met with nods of agreement from the group.

"Among your team will be all the specialists you will need," she said. "Trust each other, and you will succeed.

"This is not strictly a military mission, though it is being led by military officers. Please raise your hand as I call out your name and introduce you."

Captain Ivanov began by introducing the leader of the eight person team, Colonel Kevin Michaels.

"Ladies and gentlemen, as most of you are already acquainted, it's my pleasure to reintroduce Colonel Michaels, a familiar face among you. With a master's degree in both psychology and philosophy, Colonel Michaels is an expert in human relationships. His twenty-four years of military experience in the American Marines have also proven his leadership ability. As your team's leader and documentarian, he will be responsible for recording every discovery, speculation, and conclusion you make during your long mission.

"Colonel Michaels will meet with each of you on a daily basis to document everything you encounter, on paper and electronically, using the advanced computers that will accompany you. He will de-brief us upon your return. By then, all of us will be 16 years older. Colonel Michaels is currently 44 years old; he will be 60 upon your return."

Captain Ivanov then introduced Major Arpita Patel from the Indian Air Force. "Many of you already know Major Patel, a distinguished medical doctor with 15 years of medical experience in the Indian Air Force. From setting broken bones and pulling teeth to performing appendectomies and treating heat stroke, there is no medical condition she is not prepared to handle. She is currently 38 years old and will be 54 upon her return."

The remaining members of the crew are civilians with no military rank and were introduced in order of age.

"Next and representing France in this endeavor is Mr. Julien Bernard Jr.

"At 36, Mr. Bernard is an accomplished engineering and electrical specialist. His father is the famous American Civil Rights attorney Julien Bernard, and his mother is a French astroengineer. Julien himself is an I.T. specialist and computer expert. He is also fully trained in the construction and repair of the living quarters that you will be sharing during the project."

“The next team member is 32-year-old Russian outdoorsman and marksman, Nicholas Popov. He is a professional rock climber, hunter, fisherman, and hiker, which had earned him the label of 'the ultimate survivalist.' This makes him the perfect companion for your journey.

"Mr. Popov is also trained as a back-up documentarian and writer, and he'll be working alongside Colonel Michaels to record the deeds and findings of all other members of the group.

"Mr. Popov, as one Russian to another, I’m sure I speak for everyone when I say that we are privileged to have you as a member of our group."

Everyone let out a little laugh as Mr. Popov nodded in return.

The captain continued: "Representing Canada is Denise Hannah.

“Ms. Hannah is 27 years old, with a Ph.D. in archaeology and anthropology. She will be instrumental in finding out what happened to humanity. Should we come across the people of our future, her expertise will be vital in helping us ascertain their habits and customs.

"Ms. Hannah is also a trained botanist and biologist. Part of her duties will be to examine the cell structures of the plants and animals you encounter and must rely upon for food. She will ensure that no radical changes have taken place that might make them inedible to you.”

Captain Ivanov then moved on to introduce Andrea Wong from the People's Republic of China.

“Born to an American mother and an esteemed Chinese scientist father, Ms. Wong holds a Ph.D. in Unmanned Systems Engineering, that is, she’s a drone expert. She represents both China and the United States on this mission.

"While there,” the captain explained, "your facility will be equipped with drones to be sent out to fly over the countryside and assist you in finding people; they are technologically advanced and have a range of up to 100 kilometers – or an operational radius of 50 kilometers – without needing to be recharged. These drones will send back pictures and signals to the central computer. Ms. Wong is also 27 years old.”

The next member to be introduced was Elizabeth (Liz) Dina, the representative of the United Kingdom. She is a renowned linguist; some even considered her a savant in the field.

"At 26 years old, Ms. Dina is fluent in six languages, making her quite a polyglot. I've heard that she has a real talent for picking up new languages quickly, so no matter who you encounter on your travels, Liz will be able to help you communicate with them and figure out what they are saying.

"Liz is also a trained nurse who can assist Dr. Patel in case of any need.”

The captain moved on to the last member of the team. “The final participant, William or Willie, as he prefers – Sutton, is also from the US. At the age of 25, he is the youngest member of our group.

"With a master's degree in agronomy, Mr. Sutton is an expert in soil analysis, crop management, and animal husbandry."

The captain elaborated: "During this mission, your group will need to grow its own food, and this is where Mr. Sutton becomes indispensable. A supply of victuals will be shipped with you, which should last approximately six months. However, it is impossible to send enough food along to feed eight people for 16 years.

"Hundreds of pounds of seeds will also be sent along. Mr. Sutton will plant, grow, maintain, and harvest crops; he'll need assistance from the rest of you, of course. Like Mr. Popov, Mr. Sutton is also adept at hunting and fishing. It is impossible to predict the conditions you may encounter in the future, but with two trained outdoorsmen available Mr. Sutton and Mr. Popov your group should be prepared to handle anything.

"Mr. Sutton, we welcome you aboard."

The atmosphere in the room crackled with energy as General Yadev strode back to the podium. With a quick nod to his colleagues, he signaled the start of an interactive session, opening the floor to questions. In an authoritative but inviting voice, he encouraged the members of the crew to share any questions on their minds.

No sooner had the invitation been issued than numerous hands leaped into the air. General Yadev scanned the room, his gaze falling upon Colonel Michaels. With a smile, General Yadev acknowledged him.

"General," Colonel Michaels began, "I think I speak for everyone when I say this is the most astounding thing any of us has ever heard. We understood that we had volunteered and trained for a special 16-year interstellar space flight, but not to travel through time!

"Wow! I myself am even more excited than ever to go.

"But I think it is only fair to the group to ask everyone if this 'change in mission' alters anyone's desire to participate. I would like to know if, after hearing the details of this assignment, anyone would like to reconsider their decision to go.

"After all, if our lives are going to depend on the willingness and ability of everyone else, I'd like to be confident that they are all happy to be coming along," Colonel Michaels added.

"That's an excellent question, Colonel," General Yadev responded. He paused, allowing a moment of silence to follow his words. "Knowing the actual facts about your mission, does anyone feel compelled to withdraw?"

The room grew still, and all eyes were fixed on the General. Slowly scanning the faces of each individual, he waited for someone to speak up. No hands were raised, and everyone mumbled a collective "no, not at all."

"That's very good because, at this late date, we probably would not have let anyone back out anyway. Are there any other questions?" General Yadev asked, pointing toward Dr. Patel as she raised her hand.

"What kind of medical facilities will be available to us?" Dr. Patel asked.

"In the structure where you'll be housed, there's a fully equipped medical laboratory and operating room at your disposal. We hope you never need to use it. It's stocked with antibiotics, splints, biological microscopes, scalpels, and everything from aspirin to lip balm. We've stocked all the essentials," General Yadev explained. "While this crew is young and healthy, we still acknowledge the inevitability of accidents. Therefore, we want to ensure that you're fully prepared to handle any situation that may arise by providing you with all necessary resources."

Glancing at the other raised hands, General Yadev gestured toward Julien Bernard.

"Apparently every consideration has been given to 'political correctness', Julien noted. "It seems we have representatives from every race, creed, color, and gender," Julien remarked as he looked around.

The General was quick to reply. "The people on this mission are the best in their fields, including you, Mr. Bernard. You've been selected for your abilities and nothing else. The enormous financial cost of this mission beggars the imagination. It is many times the Gross National Product of most small countries. Each nation represented here has put in tens of billions of dollars to participate.

"The United States alone has contributed hundreds of billions of dollars towards this mission, underlining the significance of this endeavor. The objective of your journey is to uncover the mystery surrounding the people of the future, and no expense has been spared.

"Also, and quite naturally, there is some suspicion among the cooperating nations. Each nation wants to be sure that all the information brought back is made available to all the other participating countries.

"You, Mr. Bernard, and the rest of you, each represent not only your own nation but humanity as a whole. You are pioneers - and will no doubt return as heroes.

General Yadev turned his attention to Denise Hannah. "Yes, Ms. Hannah?"

"General," Denise began, "I was wondering if I may ask a hypothetical question. In the event that we do make contact with future humans, would it be possible to bring one of them back with us if they wished to return?" she asked curiously.

"I wish we could, but the scientists tell us that would be impossible. Exactly 16 years and 22 days after being transported into the future, you will be blinked back here to our time. Nothing from this time will remain there, and nothing from that time can be brought back here.

"You will be provided with ink, pens and paper, which will also be transported with you. And because the ink was sent with you, it will show up in your notes. If you were to write with ink you discovered in the future, when you returned, the pages would all be blank. The paper would return, but the ink from the future would not come back with you. Whatever you encounter there stays there, and there is nothing anyone can do about it."

With a subtle gesture, General Yadev singled out Mr. Popov, the Russian delegate.

"If I will be expected to hunt and fish, will I have a say in the weapons I take along?" Mr. Popov inquired politely.

"No, I'm afraid not, Mr. Popov," General Yadev replied. "You and Mr. Sutton will both be provided with 30-06 caliber rifles, along with hundreds of cartridges. There will be a .50-caliber rifle available to the group should you run into a brontosaurus or something. And a couple of shotguns, should they be needed for hunting small game. Colonel Michaels will be given a .45 automatic pistol. Every member of the crew will be issued tasers. Since we are not exactly sure what you might run into, everyone will be expected to carry a taser at all times."

Pointing to Andrea Wong, General Yadev gave her the floor.

"I don't want to sound vain, but what will be provided, and what will we be able to take with us, in the order of personal items? You know, makeup, hair coloring, and so forth. I mean, sixteen years is quite a stretch, and I might need a fair amount of dye for my prematurely graying hair," Andrea Wong inquired with a grin.

Andrea's question sparked laughter and concurring nods from the other women.

"Every member will be allowed to carry 75 pounds of 'personal items,'" replied the general. "These may include hair care products, makeup, books, a guitar, or whatever else you like. However, it costs roughly one hundred thousand dollars per pound to send items into the future. Your allowance of 75 pounds of personal items is costing taxpayers 7.5 million dollars per person. I'm afraid some personal care items may have to be excluded.

"Our team spent years deciding which items to take and which to leave behind. We wanted to provide you with everything, but the items you described are being sent in only limited quantities. You will be provided with 16 years' worth of soap, shampoos, deodorants, nail clippers, feminine hygiene products, and toilet paper. You, however, are free to take what you like as long as you stay under your 75-pound allowance. Remember, every pound counts," General Yadev emphasized.

The general paused, then continued, "We spent an inordinate amount of effort researching what sort of clothing to send along. You will not be stuck wearing any sort of uniform for 16 years. We have provided a variety of clothing for both the men and the women. We've taken precautions to include items appropriate for the changing seasons. In your provisions you will find a variety of clothing styles and we have taken into account the predictable expansion of waist sizes as each of you gets older. But you will undoubtedly be forced into a monotony of wearing the same items many times over."

Waiving his fingers toward the females and smiling, he continued: "A problem more likely to bother the women than the men."

His eyes turned to William Sutton. "Yes, Mr. Sutton?"

"Excuse me, General, but I doubt if I'm going to need 75 pounds worth of personal gear. Can I give some of my weight allowance to another person if I want to?" Willie asked, throwing a playful wink towards Liz.

"If you choose to give up some of your personal weight allowance, I believe it would be best that it be put in a common pool and divided equally among the remainder of the crew," General Yadev advised.

"Alright, one last question." Glancing around the room again, the general responded, "Yes, Ms. Dina?"

"I noticed that there are four males and four females going away to live in close company with each other for 16 years. Is it expected that couples will eventually be formed? What if two people fall in love? Can they get married?" Liz inquired.

"Absolutely not! To be frank with you, Liz, I fought hard to assemble a crew entirely of males for the very reasons you mentioned. Unfortunately, extensive studies indicate that a group of only males living in close quarters for years becomes unstable, often violent, and even sociopathic.

"We then considered sending only females on this journey. However, females outside the company of males develop their own set of problems. They become neurotic and unreliable. Intensive research into this subject determined conclusively that a mixture of almost equal numbers of males and females provides the most stable, cohesive, and hard-working mini-societies.

"But let's be frank. You are all relatively young people. It would be unrealistic to assume that nothing is ever going to happen between any of you. And the way I see you and young Willie acting in the break room, I suspect things have already progressed along that path.

"But I discourage it.

"Neither Colonel Michaels nor anyone else has the power to declare a couple married.

“The normal laws of civil society are not suspended for you. You are to become a society between yourselves.

"Among the strictest orders you are given, and among the most vital duties Colonel Michaels is tasked with, is to ensure that every member takes a contraceptive tablet each and every week for the next 16 years.

"A pill has been formulated by collaborating Japanese scientists that works equally well on both men and women to temporarily obstruct fertility. Each of you must take one pill a week. The pill has been fortified with vitamins and minerals. Therefore, even if you are not intimately involved with anyone, taking the pill will help ensure you stay healthy.

"In addition to the order to take one of these pills every week, you are all also required to wear your dog tags every day. Do not remove them. Even though Colonel Michaels and Dr. Patel are the only military personnel on this mission, dog tags have been made for each of you, and you must keep them on at all times. That is an order."

The general then informed the group that the next step of their training would begin after lunch and was intended to familiarize them with the housing unit that would be transported 9,100 years into the future, with them inside of it.

Back row, left to right: General Yadev, Colonel Michaels, Julien Bernard, Nicholas Popov, William Sutton
Front row, left to right: Dr. Arpita Patel, Andrea Wong, Denise Hannah, Elizabeth Dina, Dr. Schmitt

Chapter 4

The Departure

After lunch, Captain Ivanov and General Yadev introduced the team to the facility that would house them for the next 16 years and explained everything it had to offer in the way of their long term security and comfort.

Captain Ivanov began:

"In the central facility, constructed of specially designed lightweight yet durable materials, each of the eight members will have their own sleeping area measuring 8 x 10 feet. Each area is equipped with a bed, a small desk with a mirror, a chair, and a clothing storage closet. Additionally, within the central dome, there are facilities such as a kitchen, a community room, and an area for records-keeping.

"The compound is powered by a self-contained nuclear generator, meaning you'll have a seemingly infinite amount of power available to you, though we do not expect you will need more electricity than is required to heat and cool your facility, recharge the batteries in your equipment, and power your microwave oven."

As the group listened closely to Captain Ivanov's words, she went on to describe the amenities of the compound.

"There is a small gym equipped with exercise equipment and a community room with couches where you can watch movies together. There are 2,500 different movies, documentaries, television programs, and recorded musical performances to keep you entertained. This sounds like a lot, but you will be gone for over 5,800 days. My guess is that you will end up watching most of them two or three times."

Captain Ivanov then pointed out two smaller facilities attached to the main structure. "One serves as a medical station and science laboratory while the other is designated for storage of essentials like four-wheelers, grain, extra clothing, and tools.

"Within forty-eight hours of your return in 16 years, the next probe will be ready to be sent off. However, it will not be launched from the same location, as the goal is to explore as many places as possible. The probe following yours will be launched from a location 75 miles from here."

Captain Ivanov stepped aside as General Yadev returned to the front.

"Your group is being launched from the southern United States, an area known to have been inhabited for thousands of years. We expect that the people of the future will find this area equally hospitable. If there are people in the future, they should be living nearby.

"Colonel Michaels' personal area has its own bathroom and shower. This will serve as a backup showering facility for everyone in case something goes wrong with the main showering area. The rest of you will use a community shower and bathroom. Of course, repair equipment is provided for all living areas, and

Mr. Bernard has been fully trained in maintaining everything. He will be available to assist in such situations."

The general then went on to inform the crew of the "safe room" located in the center of the facility.

"It is a windowless, fully secure, sealed room and retreat, measuring 14 x 14 feet, surrounded by two-inch stainless-steel walls, floors, and ceilings. This room can be used for any purpose you desire but must remain clear of debris. It is provided as a refuge from anything that might threaten you, from tornadoes and hurricanes to bombs, poison gas, and angry mobs.

"Who knows what the people of tomorrow may think when you show up? They may be hostile. You can close yourselves in the room for as long as necessary until any danger passes.

"Outside, and attached to the facility, are three separate animal pens. Accompanying you on this journey will be a small number of Ouessant sheep and Meishan pigs. These are dwarf strains provided to us by the nations of France and the Peoples Republic of China, creatures that will remain small and easy to handle. As there are so few of you, large herds of any animal will be impossible to maintain. There will also be fourteen chickens, ten rabbits, and four small dogs."

"Psst, Willie, did you catch that? We are even provided with pets," Liz smiled in a whisper.

"Part of Mr. Sutton's duties will involve caring for these animals.

"Upon your arrival in the future, he will feed the rabbits and chickens local grasses and insects and then hand one or two of them over to Ms. Hannah and Dr. Patel for dissection and examination. After the rabbits and chickens have survived for at least a month on the local grains and grasses, he will cut up a couple more of them and feed them to the dogs to confirm that their meat is still edible and nutritious.

"Should the animals survive and prove edible after living off of local foodstuffs, you will be able to breed and raise the remainder of them for your own consumption," he asserted.

"Awww, poor bunnies," Liz whispered with a smirk.

"My grandmother was from Martinique. She used to make rabbit stew for us in France every Easter," Julien interjected with a laugh. "I'm definitely taking her recipe with us."

The general continued, "This concludes two years of extensive training. This evening, you will return to your own quarters to enjoy your last night in the 21st century. Tomorrow, at 9 AM sharp, you'll step into your facility. It will then be surrounded by a high-density Feynman Energy Field and as best we can determine, without experiencing a blip, bump, or noise, you will be instantaneously blinked into the future where you will spend the next 16 years of your lives.

"Let's all try to get a good night's sleep, and I'll see you tomorrow," General Yadev concluded.

As the group exited the building, Willie leaned in close to Liz and whispered softly, "Are you coming over to my place tonight so we can spend our last night on earth together?"

"Definitely! I'm too nervous to spend it alone," Liz responded. "But it's not our last night on earth. We'll still be on earth; it will just be a future earth."

"It will be no earth we ever knew," Willie grinned.

They all returned to their living quarters that night and tossed and turned, none of them getting much sleep. The mission was too incredible to be true. And each of them reflected that it was doubly incredible that they were the lucky ones chosen to participate.

The next morning, the group was greeted by General Yadev and Dr. Schmitt, both dressed in civilian clothes.

"Hope you all had a good night's rest," General Yadev said as he greeted the group.

"I tossed and turned all night. I think I'm over-excited. Or maybe. I'm a little bit scared and afraid to admit it," Colonel Michaels remarked.

"I gotta say, I'm a bit scared here, and I'm not afraid to admit it," Denise Hannah agreed.

"Please pay special attention to the chronometer on the wall of your facility," the general said, pointing up to the wall. "It's a uniquely designed digital timepiece that activates automatically upon your arrival in the future. It counts down the years, days and hours until your return.

"Check this chronometer at any time, and you will see just how much time you have left in the future and how much time remains before you're transported back," General Yadev explained.

TIME REMAINING				
YEARS	***DAYS***	***HOURS***	***MINUTES***	***SECONDS***
16	***22***	***0***	***0***	***0***

General Yadev and Dr. Schmitt stood at the door, and shook each person's hand warmly, thanking them sincerely and wishing them good luck.

As the last of the crew members entered, General Yadev stepped forward and cleared his throat. His voice took on a softer, more personal tone, "I've come here today not in my uniform, but in civilian clothes. I'm seeing you off, not as a general officer, but as a friend and a fellow member of the human race. I want to congratulate you before you depart and wish you the best of luck. Our thoughts and prayers will be with you."

He gestured towards the clock on the wall and continued, "Just sit back and watch the chronometer on the wall. When it changes, you will have been transported into the future." With that, the general turned around and walked away.

All eight crew members filed into the compound, each of them turning back to take one last look at the cranes, lights, cables, and about a dozen clipboard-carrying scientists that encircled the facility. The eight filed in quietly, the last one in closing the door. They each took a seat and sat motionless, their hearts beating fast with anticipation. A few moments passed when Nicholas broke the silence.

"This is it, guys. Let's do this!" he smiled.

All eyes turned to the chronometer. Almost immediately, it began to move, counting down the seconds until their mission would end.

TIME REMAINING				
YEARS	***DAYS***	***HOURS***	***MINUTES***	***SECONDS***
16	***21***	***23***	***59***	***22***

"Does this mean it happened?" Denise wondered.

"I felt nothing," Dr. Patel shrugged.

Colonel Michaels stood up from his chair, walked towards the front door, and opened it. He looked out, expecting to once again see the bustling compound that housed the noisy research facility. But to his surprise, all he saw was a serene landscape of green grass, tall trees, and blue skies. The enormous building that had housed their facility only a moment ago, along with the dozens of people running around in white lab coats, had vanished.

"It happened. We're there. Or maybe I should say 'we're here'," Colonel Michaels exclaimed.

The group was thrilled and rushed outside, unable to contain their excitement. As they looked around, they couldn't help but mutter in collective astonishment, "I can't believe it!"

At last, the wait was over; the moment they had been training for, for years, had arrived.

Chapter 5

The Sabotage

TIME REMAINING				
YEARS	***DAYS***	***Hours***	***Minutes***	***Seconds***
15	***327***	***16***	***19***	***21***

After recovering from their amazement, the crew settled down to acquaint themselves with their new surroundings. They easily managed to establish some order in their little community. To ensure everyone's safety, Colonel Michaels implemented a rule: for the first three weeks, no one was allowed to travel more than 1000 meters from the compound alone. After all, nobody knew what might be out there.

Despite their initial trepidation, the crew quickly adjusted to their new surroundings. Willie Sutton had been the busiest of them all. He got to work straight away on tilling the land for their garden, planting seeds, and feeding the sheep, pigs, chickens and rabbits on locally sourced grains and grasses.

Andrea Wong and Denise Hannah were well acquainted and had been working closely together from the start. Andrea was busy sending her drones out to survey the countryside while Denise assisted in reviewing the photos and analyzing the plant life. Together, they meticulously searched for any signs of human activity. So far, they had found nothing. But they had only just begun.

Nicholas Popov had been helping Willie Sutton as much as he could but, frustrated by the safety precautions, he kept bugging Colonel Michaels for permission to travel further from the compound to explore their surroundings. He was certain that there was a whole lot more to this area than what they had seen so far, and he was eager to discover it.

It had been two long months since the team's arrival. Dr. Patel had been working tirelessly, dissecting and examining the animals, leaving no stone unturned in her relentless pursuit to ensure the safety of the team. Finally, after weeks of hard work, she gave the green light and announced that the animals were safe to eat!

The team sat around the dinner table, their stomachs growled with hunger as they eagerly awaited the feast that Colonel Michaels and Dr. Patel had prepared for them.

Colonel Michaels skillfully took a steaming dish off the stove and placed it gently on the table.

"I hope you all like it," he remarked, meeting the eyes of each team member. "Dr. Patel and I have been cooking up a storm with the food that was sent along with us from the past. Tonight, we have prepared lasagna and salmon for you all to enjoy."

The team wasted no time diving into the spread, savoring each bite as if it were a sentimental taste of home. Colonel Michaels then brought up an important topic. "Beginning tomorrow, we need to start transitioning to local fare," he said. "Nicholas, do you and Willie think you can head into the woods and bring back some game?"

"There is a small creek full of ducks located about a mile north of here," said Nicholas. "They seem completely unafraid of humans. I bet I could walk within ten feet of them before they'd fly away. What do you say Willie? Shall we go duck hunting tomorrow?"

Willie was obviously not looking forward to going with Nicholas. Something was bugging him.

"I suppose," Willie responded hesitantly.

"I think I speak for everyone when I say things are getting a little boring around here," Liz interjected. "It's only been a couple of months, and what have we seen? Trees and grass, that's it! It's like Mother Nature hit repeat on the forest channel."

"We've got a treasure trove of work ahead of us!" Dr. Patel responded. "There's a whole world waiting to be uncovered, and we're just getting warmed up. Once we crack the code on finding all the people, I'm sure things will heat up and become very exciting."

Another month went by, and there was still no trace of human activity. After Colonel Michaels had recorded all the data collected each day, he lay down on his bed in the dim light of his small room and contemplated the situation. It had become obvious to the colonel that Nicholas was not the only one who was feeling restless.

"It's far too early to give up hope," he said to himself. "Everyone expected to get here and find the place crawling with people. It isn't. I'm going to have to work on a safe plan to expand our search, just as Nicholas suggested."

Back in December, 2042, Dr. Schmitt urgently requested a meeting with General Yadev. The General, visibly intrigued by the serious nature of the request, agreed to meet with Dr. Schmitt immediately.

Dr. Schmitt stood at the open door of General Yadev's office, a worried expression on her face.

"Come in, Dr. Schmitt," the general beckoned, lifting his gaze from his paperwork. "You've requested a meeting with me? What's the problem, and why the urgency?"

"General, I've got some startling news," Dr. Schmitt stated, settling into the chair opposite the general's desk. "After the *Timenell* crew left, my team has been busy reviewing every detail. We wanted to confirm that everything got off safely, and as you know, there are thousands of individual details to check."

"Yes, what is it?" General Yadev inquired, leaning forward in his seat. "Get to the point, doctor. What's the problem?"

"Well, General, you might remember the name of Wayne Sharon," Dr. Schmitt began cautiously. "He was in the final running for selection of the crew of *Timenell*."

"Yes, I vaguely remember him. He was eliminated, wasn't he? He was replaced by Willie Sutton, as I recall," the general mused.

"That's right," Dr. Schmitt nodded. "He didn't pass the final psychological tests. Well, apparently, he didn't take the news too well. To placate him, we added him to the mission's procurement team. The procurement team was responsible for filling all the supply requirements and loading them into the compound. After he began requisitioning the materials for the *Timenell* crew, he decided to use his new position to take a little revenge for having been replaced."

"Revenge? What do you mean, revenge?" General Yadev's voice hardened.

"As you know, sir, part of the supplies for the eight-member team were unisex contraceptive tablets. Well, it seems that Mr. Sharon wanted to play a sick joke and he replaced all the pills with simple vitamin tablets. In effect, he has attempted to sabotage our mission."

The general's features darkened with rage as he reflected upon the severity of the situation.

"He has been arrested and is being charged right now," Dr. Schmitt added quickly.

She then spelled it out. "What this means is that we didn't actually send any contraceptive pills along with the team. We sent 45,000 simple vitamin tablets instead. The crew has no birth control, and they don't even know it."

General Yadev, more than perturbed, sighed and tousled his hair with his hand.

“What do you think is going to happen, General?” Dr. Schmitt wondered out loud.

"Who knows! What can we expect? Maybe nothing will happen. I don't know. God only knows… Maybe God doesn’t even know," he spat out.

Chapter 6

The Tragedy

TIME REMAINING				
YEARS	***DAYS***	***HOURS***	***MINUTES***	***SECONDS***
15	***287***	***15***	***18***	***1***

Colonel Michaels strolled up behind Andrea and Denise, his gaze fixed on the contents of their computer screen.

"Andrea, any luck with the drone search? Any signs of human life or activity popping up?" Colonel Michaels inquired.

Andrea shook her head. "No, Colonel, I'm afraid not," she stated with marked disappointment. "As you know, the drones we've been provided with can travel many kilometers out and back. They transmit audio and visual data to me every step of the way. I can record and review everything they see in visual, infrared, and ultraviolet light.

“That's close to 2500 square kilometers of detailed searching. And yet, so far, I've found nothing – not the tiniest trace of any human activity.

“We have been scouring the local area for over three months now, if people did live nearby, they are long gone. There are no traces of trails, roads, buildings, skeletal remains, nothing. It seems humans have not lived anywhere near here for centuries."

"We've come across plenty of Pinus Palustris and Platanus Occidentalis in abundance, with slightly higher densities than when we left, but nothing out of the ordinary to report," Denise chimed in.

"What are you saying, Denise? What is Pinus ... whatever?" Colonel Michaels asked.

"Apologies, Colonel. What I meant to convey is that we've come across plenty of pine and sycamore trees, but not much beyond that," Denise explained.

Colonel Michaels pointed his finger into the air as if having an epiphany. “Maybe we should conduct the search at night; maybe the people here are nocturnal for some reason.”

“I’ve already been doing that, Colonel” Andrea responded. “The problem is getting someone to review all the footage that comes with a 24-hour-a-day search. The computers can help us, but Denise and I can only stare into these screens for so long before our eyes begin to feel like they are falling out!”

Julien, who had entered the room a few minutes earlier and overheard their conversation, intervened. “What do we do if we continue to search the area for the next few weeks and still find nothing?” Julien asked, posing the question to anyone who might have an answer.

“Nicholas and I have worked together to develop a plan to expand our physical search beyond the five-kilometer limit we initially established for ourselves,” replied Colonel Michaels. “We will begin expanding our search on foot, looking for clues.

“If nothing is found, Andrea will take the drones and launch them from places farther away from our compound. We will expand their search past the 50-kilometer range.

“We have been provided with some lightweight camping gear and four battery-operated four-wheelers. Andrea will just have to expand her search farther and farther beyond the local area. We must keep going until we find some human activity," the Colonel added.

Denise stepped in. "The four-wheelers we've been given aren't exactly speed demons. Plus, with no roads in sight, if Andrea is to travel a long distance from our location, just getting

there and back may take many hours.”

"When it comes time to physically travel and explore on foot beyond the 5-kilometer range, the men will take turns traveling out with Andrea and maybe staying out there overnight,” Colonel Michaels stated.

Denise bristled. "Hey now that sounds a bit sexist. I think the women can take turns going out with Andrea, too. After all, we are all trained to use the guns that we have been provided with," Denise replied.

Andrea leaned over and whispered to Denise, "I appreciate the sentiment, but I think I'd rather go camping with the men."

Denise chuckled, “Yeah, but we don’t want them to know that!”

Later that night, at dinner, the room was filled with chatter and the clinking of cutlery against plates.

Willie, who was sitting next to Liz just as he had done at every meal for the past three months, slipped his hand beneath the table onto her leg. She immediately brushed his hand away, jumped up, picked up her plate, and announced:

"Excuse me, I think I want to change the place I sit at mealtime. Will anyone change seats with me?"

By this time, it had become apparent to everyone that Liz and Nicholas were attracted to each other. Every day, they seemed to find some excuse to do things with each other and were often seen talking and laughing together. It was clear that their behavior was irritating Willie. Liz’s request was followed by a few seconds of uncomfortable silence.

Sensing the unease, Denise piped up, "I'll trade places with you," and they swapped seats.

The next morning, Willie and Nicholas got up early to go duck hunting. As they walked through the woods, Nicholas turned to Willie and said:

"You know, my friend, you shouldn't get so attached to women. They come, and they go, and then after a while, they come back again."

"What are you talking about?" Willie questioned.

"You and Liz, everyone knows you two were an item. I repeat, **'were'** an item. And now everyone knows there is some problem between you. In a tiny group like ours, secrets don't really stay for long. Do not be heartbroken," Nicholas commented.

"Just mind your own business," Willie retorted sharply.

As they were setting up their equipment, a pair of ducks flew over their heads. In an instant, reacting as if from instinct, both men raised their shotguns and fired. With a resounding bang, both ducks plummeted from the sky, landing with a thud.

Nicholas, laughing out loud, said, "Looks like you're better at getting birds than keeping chicks, Willie!"

"Just leave me alone! You're not funny!" Willie snapped, clearly annoyed.

Nicholas's incessant teasing, particularly since the brush-off he received from Liz the previous evening, was eating away at him. He was convinced that Nicholas was trying to seduce Liz and it seemed like she was not all that keen on resisting. Inside, Willie was fuming.

Early the next morning, Willie got up from the breakfast table to attend to his daily routine of weeding the garden and feeding the livestock. He was deep in thought and didn't say anything to the colonel as he left the table.

Colonel Michaels, who had been sitting across the table from him reading a book, spoke up. "See you later, Willie."

Willie looked over, as if startled out of a daze and responded,

"Oh yeah, I'll see you later, Colonel."

A moment later, Andrea and Julien appeared and sat down for breakfast. "What are you reading, Colonel?" Julien asked.

"It's a philosophy book titled, *Our Human Herds*, it's very interesting," the colonel replied.

"My tastes run more along the lines of engineering," Julien responded.

"Well," said the colonel, "philosophy is sort of like an investigation into human engineering – why we do what we do and believe what we believe that sort of thing."

"Let me ask you two something," the colonel continued. "Is the tension between Willie, Liz, and Nicholas as obvious to you two as it is to me?"

Andrea was first to respond. "Liz loves the attention from both men. But it is clear her feelings for Willie, whatever they once were, are not as strong as her feelings for Nicholas. You can't be in the same room with her without her bringing up something about Nicholas. If she's not in love with him, she sure is acting like she is in front of the girls."

Julien nodded his head and added, "Nicholas has been my close friend since our training began. He is a funny, sarcastic, egomaniac, but he is a really nice guy. He is a jokester and a pain in the ass sometimes; but he's a nice guy."

As he stepped outside, Willie ran into Nicholas, who was looking for Liz.

"Hey Willie, have you seen Liz around?" Nicholas asked.

Willie pretended not to hear him and continued walking.

Nicholas smirked sarcastically, and with a theatrical flourish, flexed his arm muscles, the veins popping out as he yelled out, "Hey Willie, I think Liz has decided she likes brawn over brains."

"You Russians really are pieces of crap. Leave me the hell alone," Willie muttered, stinging from the taunt.

To Colonel Michaels, who felt responsible for maintaining harmony and a spirit of cooperation among the team members, the situation that was developing between Liz, Willie, and Nicholas was a source of concern. Willie was becoming increasingly angry and withdrawn because of the obvious attraction between Liz and Nicholas. And the more it bothered Willie, the more Nicholas seemed to enjoy it. It seemed to the colonel like the two men were on the verge of coming to blows over Liz. He hoped they were mature enough to handle the situation, but he had his doubts.

“I may soon have to speak to them,” he thought to himself.

The next morning, as Willie was walking out of the compound carrying a shotgun, Colonel Michaels looked up from the book he was reading and asked, "Where are you off to, Willie?"

"I'm going to shoot some ducks and get my mind off my problems," Willie responded.

As he headed along the footpath towards the creek, his worst fears were confirmed. Just around a bend, not far from the front door of the compound but partially concealed by bushes, he came upon Liz and Nicholas in a passionate embrace. Things were obviously well past the flirtation stage.

Willie ran over to Liz and pulled her away from Nicholas, exclaiming, "Why are you doing this? This guy is a piece of shit!

You know I'm the one who loves you!"

Liz jerked herself away from Willie and yelled sharply, "Get off my case! I'm not your property. Leave me alone!"

Shocked and paralyzed with fury, Willie stood there, clenching his fist. Finally, he turned and took a few steps back yelling, "Screw both of you! If you prefer a guy with big muscles and a small brain, you found the right man."

Unphased by Willie's outburst, and clearly the winner in the competition for Liz's affections, Nicholas smiled and replied sarcastically, "Don't let it bother you, mate. I'm sure she'll be thinking of you every time she is in my arms."

In a moment of blind rage, Willie pointed the gun at Nicholas and fired. In an explosion of sound and blood, Nicholas collapsed to the ground. Liz screamed in horror. Recognizing the magnitude of his actions and immediately regretting them, Willie staggered away and sat down on the ground.

"Oh God, what have I done? Oh my God!" Willie mumbled in sweating tearful distress.

Nicholas lay on the ground squirming in a pool of his own blood with Liz wailing over him.

"Help, help, please help! Doctor Patel, please help! Oh God, someone help! He's been shot! Please, someone, anyone, do something!" Liz cried out.

Everyone inside the compound heard the shot and the commotion and came running out.

"What the hell happened!!?" Colonel Michaels thundered.

"Willie... he... he shot Nicholas! Oh, please help him," Liz screamed as she fell to her knees next to Nicholas's squirming body.

Julien turned to Colonel Michaels. "I hope the kid tells us that this was an accident."

Colonel Michaels took charge, his voice commanding. "Julien, help me get Nicholas inside immediately. Dr. Patel, please come with us to the medical center. The rest of you, see to Liz."

Colonel Michaels and Julien lifted Nicholas's limp body, carrying him swiftly into the medical center. They carefully placed him on the examination table, where his labored breathing could be heard along with some incoherent mumbling as he gurgled in his own blood. Julien, too upset to stay, quickly left the room.

"Right now, I really need a nurse, and Liz, who's trained for this, is too upset," Dr. Patel lamented.

Liz remained outside kneeling on the ground crying, unable to process what she had just witnessed, refusing to stand, as if standing would force her to deal with what had occurred.

"She's in no shape to help you with this. Just tell me what you need, and I'll try to help," Colonel Michaels responded.

The crew had been provided with some strong anesthesia, and Dr. Patel injected some into Nicholas's near lifeless body. She was hoping to ease his pain. She had not yet fully examined the wound, she knew it was serious, but held out hope that something could be done. A couple of minutes later she turned to the colonel shaking her head slowly.

"I need no more help; he's dead," Dr. Patel announced quietly. "Before I got a good look at the wound, I hoped there would be something that could be done. After I examined him more closely, I recognized that it hardly mattered. I don't care if we were back home in the middle of the most well-equipped hospital in the world. With a hole that big in the center of his body, there was no way he was going to survive."

There was a long pause as both of them stared down at Nicholas's dead body. Then they looked up at each other.

"What are you going to do now? About Willie, I mean?" Dr. Patel inquired.

Colonel Michaels shrugged. "I wish I knew. You tell me," he replied, in a tone somewhere between anger, confusion, and misery.

The colonel returned to the main area where Andrea, Denise, and Julien were consoling Liz, who continued to sob uncontrollably.

He took a deep breath, and in a solemn voice, addressed the four of them. "I regret having to tell you this, but Nicholas is dead." Liz wailed, and the others gasped in shock.

Colonel Michaels grabbed Julien's arm and motioned him to come into the medical laboratory.

"Let's carry Nicholas out back," Colonel Michaels urged. "There is an area of soft ground about 100 feet from the compound where we can bury him."

"What are you going to do about this, Colonel?" Julien inquired.

"You think I know? I must have missed the training session where they taught me what to do when the crew begins to kill each other...Let's get going. Pick him up," Colonel Michaels instructed.

Chapter 7

What Is Justice?

TIME REMAINING				
YEARS	***DAYS***	***HOURS***	***MINUTES***	***SECONDS***
15	***285***	***14***	***10***	***13***

The two men struggled with the heavy body, their movements labored as they carried it to the rear of the compound. They started digging a hole, the shovel cutting into the earth with each stroke. As they put Nicholas's body in and began covering it with dirt, Andrea appeared.

“I’ve been a devout Christian ever since my mom told me about the horrors that Christians endured in China. I brought a Bible along as part of my personal belongings. Is it alright if I say a prayer over him?” Andrea asked.

“Yes, of course,” Colonel Michaels rejoined.

"Please do," Julien urged.

Andrea offered a prayer, her words carrying softly over the solemn scene. With Nicholas laid to rest, the men completed the burial rites and returned inside, their thoughts heavy with the weight of their loss.

Julien, looking about as sad as a man can look, turned to the colonel and said, “Now I know why, when a person dies, they no longer say ‘this is Nicholas’; they say instead, ‘this is Nicholas’s body.’ When you see a person dead, whom you knew and loved when they were alive, you realize there’s something missing. That wasn’t Nicholas we buried. It was Nicholas’s body.”

“Now it is you who is sounding religious…or philosophical,” Colonel Michaels remarked.

Returning to the main compound, Colonel Michaels addressed those gathered in the kitchen area.

"Where are Liz and Willie?" he inquired.

"They've both gone into their rooms," Denise replied.

"That's good. I want everyone to go about their duties as best they can. I just need a little time to mull this over. After dinner tonight, we'll gather for a meeting. I expect everyone to be prepared to share their thoughts on this matter. Between now and then, I want Willie and Liz to remain in their rooms. Denise, please convey this message to them. I'll speak with them individually in a few minutes to get their stories."

In a short time, Colonel Michaels tapped on Liz’s bedroom door, stepped in, and settled beside her on the bed, doing his best to project support, comfort, and reassurance.

"Elizabeth, pull yourself together and give me the facts as best you can remember them. Start at the beginning. What happened between you, Willie, and Nicholas?" Colonel Michaels inquired.

“Well, Willie and I have been close friends since we started training for this mission, but I’ve realized for some time that my feelings for him are not as strong as his feelings for me. I never wanted to have an exclusive relationship with him. After we arrived here Nicholas started flirting with me, and I became strongly attracted to him. Willie could sense this, and it made him angry. And I began to resent his possessiveness.

“To make matters worse, Nicholas seemed to get some pleasure teasing Willie about it. I asked him to stop it, but he continued. I do not think either of us realized how badly it affected Willie. At first, I tried to be discreet I was trying to avoid a confrontation with Willie but Nicholas refused to tiptoe around and said it would ultimately be better for Willie to face reality. I think most of the others in our group were aware that something was going on between me and Nicholas. But Willie … I don’t know. He clearly sensed something and was angry, but I think he was holding out hope that nothing significant had really happened yet until, of course, he stumbled upon me embracing Nicholas.”

"So, what happened then?" Colonel Michaels inquired.

"Willie had his gun with him. He had planned to go hunting. When he saw me and Nicholas kissing, he rushed over and yanked me away; I was annoyed, and I told him to back off.

“Willie could see that I was not going to listen to him, and he turned around as if to storm off. Nicholas sort of stepped toward him," Liz explained.

"Did Nicholas try to fight with Willie or hurt him?” the Colonel questioned.

"No." Liz responded, almost in a whisper. "He was sort of teasing Willie. But he didn't mean anything by it. Willie yelled something back at us, and Nicholas began yelling something back at him. I thought they might get into a fight, but I never thought Willie would shoot him."

Liz put her head in her hands, overwhelmed with grief. “I think I was falling in love with Nicholas. He is the first man I ever really felt that way about. I do love him...” she trailed off and buried her face, covered in tears, into the pillow on her bed.

“Do you think this was premeditated, Liz?” the colonel asked.

"I know Willie didn't mean it,” she sobbed. “He didn’t plan it. But Nicholas is still dead. Oh, how can I even say those words!?”

Liz couldn’t stop crying. She felt like she was going insane with grief.

After leaving Liz’s room, Colonel Michaels knocked on Willie's door. The colonel could hear Willie sniffling on the other side. After a few moments, Willie opened the door and invited the colonel to come in. The colonel sat down on a chair next to the small desk, while Willie sat on his bed facing him, with a look of both anxiety and despair. Both of them paused and seemed to be deep in thought, perhaps contemplating what they were dealing with and what, if anything, could justify what happened.

The colonel asked Willie to recount the tragic events from the time he left the compound. The factual details of Willie's account matched what Liz had just told him.

"Did Nicholas make any threatening gestures toward you?" the colonel asked.

"No, I guess not," Willie confessed; and after a pause, added, "unless you consider stealing someone's girlfriend and taunting them about it a 'threatening gesture'."

"Not sufficiently threatening to kill them," the colonel replied, gently prodding Willie to further explain his reaction.

"Oh God, I know!" Willie blurted out in a quivering voice as he turned away from the colonel to wipe the tears from his eyes. "I don't know what came over me. It all happened so fast. I had a sleepless night last night, upset about Liz's moving away from me at the supper table. When I came upon them kissing this morning, it confirmed my worst fears, and when he started teasing me, I lost it. All I was aware of was the anger boiling in me. I honestly don't even remember shooting the gun or hearing the sound it made. It was like some evil spirit had taken over my body."

His voice cracked. "I never meant to kill him; I swear. I even liked him sometimes. I don't know how I am going to live with myself."

Colonel Michaels patted Willie on the shoulder and exited the bedroom, walking slowly to join the others at the kitchen table. Everyone seemed to be in a state of shock. He suggested that they all disperse to their individual rooms and reconvene in two hours without Willie and Liz. The group nodded in agreement, and everyone got up from the table and retreated to their respective quarters.

Two hours later, the group made their way back around the kitchen table.

"The reason for our gathering," Colonel Michael emphasized, "is to review the circumstances surrounding the death of our friend, Nicholas."

Julien wasted no time in leveling an accusation. "Straight-up murder," he declared resolutely. "Willie murdered Nicholas. That's the bottom line; end of story!"

Denise wasn't buying into Julien's straightforward view. She offered a more nuanced approach.

"It's not exactly that cut-and-dry. Willie had no intention of hurting anyone when he walked outside, and he was provoked. He did kill Nicholas, but there were mitigating circumstances."

"Yeah, Denise, but come on," Julien shot back, "provoked or not, he still crossed a line. You can't just brush that off."

Denise shook her head. "I'm not brushing it off, Julien. I'm just saying we need to assess all the factors before we make any judgments."

Julien scoffed. "I'm sorry, but I disagree. I think it's pure murder. Back on earth… I mean, back where we came from, it would be considered murder. That's all there is to it. Now, how do we address this situation?" Julien's stance was unequivocal.

"But what does that mean – 'How do we address this situation'?" Andrea inquired. "What options do we have?"

Colonel Michaels laid it out firmly, emphasizing the vital roles played by Nicholas and Willie. "Just so we're clear, there's no jail here.

"Nicholas and Willie were the two people here who had the hardest jobs. Both worked every day to find and grow our food and take care of the animals. Now that there is only one of them, we are all twice as dependent upon Willie. We need him more than ever! We can't simply lock him in his room for the next 15 and a half years. We have to go on.

"We'll address it somehow," he continued, leaning in a bit. "We'll make sure Willie understands how serious this is. But punishment won't magically bring Nicholas back, nor will it solve our current challenges. Our focus must be on adapting and moving forward as a group."

"Well, my skills have not been in much demand since we've arrived here. I'm ready to help Willie do what needs to be done," Denise offered.

Julien nodded. "I think we will all have to do more now. But that doesn't negate the fact that Willie murdered Nicholas. We can't just sweep it under the rug and act like it never occurred. But no matter the decision we make, whether by vote or by silence, it cannot alter the truth that Nicholas, who was a good friend of mine, is dead. We owe it to him and to ourselves to tackle this head-on, regardless of how uncomfortable it gets."

"Julien," Colonel Michaels retorted, "Nicholas was a good friend to all of us. If the roles were reversed, and it had been you in that tragic situation? If it had been you who was shot in a moment of unpremeditated passion, what would you want us to do about Willie? What is justice here?"

Julien's response came after a prolonged silence. "I ... I honestly don't know. I'm not sure what to think or what we can do."

After being remarkably silent up to now, Dr. Patel spoke up. "We are not a court, and we are not a jail; but let's not forget, courts and jails will be waiting for us when we return. The only practical course of action is to inform Willie and remind ourselves that upon our return, we'll hand the matter over to the authorities. They can handle it from there. Between now and then, we all have to do our jobs, and we all have to get along. It's important that none of us looks down on others."

"I think Dr. Patel is right," the colonel affirmed. "Given the circumstances, it's best for us to treat it like we have no jurisdiction in the matter and move on."

The group listened carefully to the words of Dr. Patel and

Colonel Michaels, words that seemed quite wise at the time. After pausing to reflect, they all nodded in agreement, accepting that this was indeed the only practical solution.

Chapter 8

The Facts

TIME REMAINING				
YEARS	***DAYS***	***HOURS***	***MINUTES***	***SECONDS***
15	*277*	*11*	*21*	*5*

In the aftermath of Nicholas's death, everyone was left wondering what could be done about the terrible deed that had unfolded. The nightly ritual of watching movies together, once a comforting escape, felt hollow. That night, no one even bothered to pick a film. Everyone just went to bed early. From the next room, the sound of Liz's gentle sobbing seeped through the walls, accompanied by the faint sniffles of Willie's tears. A deep sense of loss seemed to consume the remaining members of the group, leaving them feeling helpless.

Over the next few days, Willie worked tirelessly in his garden from sunrise to sunset, barely interacting with anyone. His usual hunting trips, which he used to take almost daily, were completely forgotten. He would wake up at sunrise, roll up his sleeves, slip on his gardening gloves, and set off to work.

Willie inspected each animal and every plot of vegetables with care. But amidst his duties, he remained withdrawn and silent, focusing solely on his tasks without uttering a word.

One morning, while Willie was alone in the gardens, Colonel

Michaels decided to ask him to hunt some fresh meat for dinner.

The Colonel had been watching Willie and was concerned about his depression and stand-offish demeanor. Carrying the very shotgun that had killed Nicholas, the colonel said to him, “Willie, we’re all getting tired of chowing down on only vegetables and fish. How about you take this gun and go down to the river and bring back a half-dozen of those mallards?”

“I’m sorry, Colonel Michaels, but I have vowed never to touch a shotgun again,” Willie adamantly declared.

"I'm sure you did, son. But, right now, we need you to hunt for us. We expect nothing short of your absolute best. Take Julien along and teach him how to hunt today, and I'll go with you tomorrow. We need to put this behind us and do the best we can," Colonel Michaels insisted.

The colonel deliberately manipulated the situation so that Julien and Willie would be alone together for hours. He could not stand by and allow any walls to be built up between the two men. Creating a situation where the two men would spend hours alone together would force them to confront and overcome any animosity between them.

"I never meant to kill him, Colonel, I swear. I've never been violent towards anyone in my life," Willie stressed.

"I believe you, Willie. I always have," Colonel Michaels affirmed.

"What's going to happen to me when we return back home? What if they see only the blood on my hands? You'll all be celebrated as heroes, and I'll be branded as a murderer, won't I?" Willie inquired desperately.

"I don't know what's going to happen when we get back, my friend," Colonel Michaels replied. "But one thing I do know: if we can all go back and say that from this day forward, you were the perfect companion and a hard worker who put the good of the group ahead of his own needs, I believe it will count for something."

As the team moved on from the traumatic event, they gradually began to notice a shift in the formerly strained environment. Days passed, and eventually the previously tense and somber mood gave way to a lighter and more positive one. The team members started sharing light-hearted jokes, trying to lift each other's spirits. It seemed like the crew was beginning to heal from the deep emotional wound that hung over them.

Willie, in particular, who had been affected by the traumatic event almost to the point of paralysis, seemed to have finally begun to bounce back to his usual self and was seen indulging in his favorite hobbies of hunting and fishing, though with diminished passion.

Initially, Liz and Willie had kept their distance from each other, but as the days passed they began spending time together again, helping each other get over the horrible event. It was almost as if they navigated their recovery together, finding strength in each other's company. Neither would mention the name of Nicholas. For Liz, mentioning his name was too painful; for Willie, it was a name he wished he had never heard in his life.

Willie made an overt and unabashed attempt to hang on Liz's every word. He laughed at all of her jokes, and took her side in every conflict. She frequently looked more annoyed than complimented over his rapt attention, but she never overtly discouraged it.

As the crew resumed their daily activities, a change in everyone's attitude toward their mission became apparent. In the shadow of Nicholas's death, it seemed that each of the remaining crew members were questioning what the hell they were doing in this seemingly uninhabited wilderness. Despondency seemed to have taken hold. Everyone in the crew appeared to be wishing that some trace of humanity would soon be found, to provide a happy distraction from the recent sad events.

One evening, as everyone made their way to the table for dinner, Andrea asked the question everyone had probably been thinking for some time. "Colonel Michaels, suppose we never find any people and are never able to figure out what happened to them?"

The colonel's direct reply seemed almost harsh. "If that were to happen, we would have spent the better part of our lives on a very long camping trip."

Chapter 9

When a Truth Cannot Be a Fact

TIME REMAINING				
YEARS	***DAYS***	***HOURS***	***MINUTES***	***SECONDS***
15	***224***	***12***	***46***	***34***

It was now two months since the death of Nicholas.

Liz had been anxious for some days. This was the second month she had missed her period. She hadn't been concerned the first month and had simply attributed it to changes in the environment or the shock of Nicholas's death. But now she had missed her second period and had been feeling nauseous for the past few mornings.

She was sure she had not forgotten to take her contraceptive pills as instructed, so she could not possibly be pregnant. She felt that it was just her imagination. After all, she volunteered for this 16-year trek, knowing that, in all probability, she was giving up her chance at motherhood.

After throwing up three days in a row, she decided to consult Dr. Patel.

She made her way through the hallway to where Dr. Patel was standing just outside her medical area.

"Dr. Patel, I need to see you in the medical center. It's important. At least, I think it may be important," Liz stated.

"Of course," replied Dr. Patel. "Let's head to the medical center right away. If you feel it's important, then it certainly warrants our attention. What seems to be the issue?"

Liz felt uncomfortable jumping right into her worries. So, she began by making some small talk.

"I was just wondering—are you a Hindu?" Liz questioned.

"Maybe I'm a little Hindu, a little Muslim, a little Buddhist, and a little Christian. Is that your problem? You want to discuss my religion?" Dr. Patel wondered.

"No. What I came here to talk to you about was… Well, I'm not really sure. But if I didn't know better, I'd think I might be pregnant," Liz blurted out.

"That's impossible, unless you forgot to take your pill of course. But even then, your young man would have had to forget to take his as well," said the doctor.

Liz shook her head emphatically, "No! That's why I'm confused."

“Well, a couple of tests will tell us for sure; they’re easy enough to perform. I’ll just take a blood sample, and you can get me a urine specimen too,” Dr. Patel instructed.

After the tests were run, Liz noticed the worried expression on Dr. Patel’s face.

“I’m afraid, my dear, that you are most definitely pregnant,” Dr. Patel confirmed.

“But how is that possible? I mean, we take those pills religiously every week. I always take mine. I’ve never missed a week,” Liz questioned.

“Clearly, something went wrong. Maybe it was stress. Maybe under so much stress, the pills do not work,” Dr. Patel mused. “But it doesn’t really matter how it happened,” she continued. “The fact remains that you are pregnant.”

Noticing the stunned expression on Liz’s face, Dr. Patel reached over and took her hand. “Don’t be nervous. Women have been having babies for a long time.”

“That’s not the only problem Dr. Patel,” Liz continued. “Don’t look down upon me, but I really don’t know whose baby it is, Nicholas’s or Willie’s.”

Dr. Patel looked away for a moment, and then turned back and looked Liz straight in the eyes.

“Don’t be foolish child,” Dr. Patel said in a firm but comforting way. “That baby belongs to Willie. It will be hard enough growing up here without other kids to play with. We need to be sure it gets as much love as possible from everyone.”

"But" said an obviously worried Liz, "What if the baby is born with blonde hair and blues eyes? Willie and I are both brunettes with brown eyes."

"I don't care if that baby is born wearing a fur hat and playing the balalaika; it's Willie's baby," Dr. Patel insisted. "Put it out of your mind that there is any other possibility."

The doctor sighed and bit her lip. "Oh my, I just don't know how I am going to break this to the colonel. He worries about everything."

"Please don't tell the colonel or anyone else just yet," begged Liz. "I need some time to break it to Willie."

"A few days more will not make any difference, I suppose," Dr. Patel agreed.

The following days found Liz going out of her way to show her attachment to Willie. She sought his company and followed him around whenever she could as he did his chores. She helped him feed the chickens and even asked him to teach her how to fish. She was by his side every minute and the two soon appeared to everybody to be inseparable.

Following the death of Nicholas, and what he imagined was the irreconcilable loss of Liz, Willie had been weighed down with despair. It had often crossed his mind to commit suicide. Knowing the crew needed him more than ever prevented him from thinking too long about it.

But lately, following quickly upon the recent enthusiastic attention he was getting from Liz, his energy returned, and his demeanor seemed to turn around completely. His grief, and it seemed to him Liz's grief, was behind them. They had found each other again and this time he felt that nothing could stand in the way.

"You know that I love you," Willie often repeated to Liz.

Liz could not have been any more assured of Willie's love, but she also felt she could never really return his love with the same intensity. She hoped her resentment toward him, over the death of Nicholas, would fade. She knew he never meant to shoot Nicholas and that he regretted it deeply.

She did her best to return every smile with a smile. "*Fake it 'till you make it,*" she often thought to herself.

A week went by, and one morning, Dr. Patel found herself alone at the kitchen table with the colonel. He was engrossed in a very large philosophy book that had captured his attention, on and off, for the past few weeks.

"What are you reading, Colonel?" the doctor began.

"Oh, good morning, Dr. Patel," the Colonel responded as he looked up from his book. "It's a very interesting philosophy book called *Our Human Herds*. It lays out something called the 'Theory of Dual Morality.' I find it fascinating. The subtitle is *'Why Right is Right, Wrong is Wrong, and How Right can Also be Wrong*."

Dr. Patel, looking serious, said "Speaking of right and wrong, can I have a word with you about Liz?"

“Of course,” said the colonel. “I noticed she and Willie have become close again, and it has made a world of difference in Willie’s mood.”

“Hmmm, yes very close indeed,” replied the doctor.

“What do you mean by that, Arpita?” asked the colonel. “You have a peculiar look on your face.”

“Well, I’m not supposed to spill the beans yet, but I think the time has come for you to know. Liz is pregnant,” Dr. Patel revealed.

“What! Are you sure?” Colonel Michaels asked incredulously, almost falling out of his chair.

“Oh, quite sure,” Dr. Patel replied.

The colonel stood up and began pacing back and forth in front of the table. “Those two are screwing things up. They have been at the center of every problem we have faced in this undertaking. I will not allow them to endanger this mission,” he muttered angrily.

“Calm down, my friend. They are not endangering the mission,” Dr. Patel promptly responded. “Both are fully capable of doing their duties. Willie is happier than I have ever seen him, and Liz can interpret languages even with a big baby bump.”

“Look, Arpita, I’m concerned about practicalities here,” Colonel Michaels said in a take-charge manner. “A baby will distract us from our mission. Boredom is already forcing us to lose focus on what we are all here for. An abortion is the only logical solution.”

"I have not discussed the possibility of an abortion with her, and she shows no interest in that," Dr. Patel responded.

"It's really the only course of action," insisted the colonel. "Can you perform one?"

"I never have, and I never will," Dr. Patel responded, in a voice every bit as insistent as the colonel's. "I will not do it, even if you order me. Consider it out of the question."

Her adamant refusal took the colonel by surprise.

The doctor stood up and returned to the medical facility. The colonel shook his head and went outside for a walk. He wanted to take a measure of the stunning news Dr. Patel had given him and think about how a baby might alter the parameters of the mission.

Later that evening, as the group began to file around the table for dinner, they heard shouts of joy echoing throughout the compound.

"This is the greatest day of my life!" they heard Willie exclaim. "I feel like I hit the lottery!"

As Liz and Willie emerged from Liz's room, everyone turned to them, wondering what was going on.

Liz took a deep breath and appeared extremely nervous. She told herself, "Alright, Liz, here goes nothing!"

"OK, everyone. Please stay seated," Liz began. "I have something to tell all of you. I know this may take you by surprise;

it certainly took me by surprise when I found out. I need to make an important announcement. The thing is, I am pregnant, and I have absolutely no clue as to how it all happened. Willie and I will be bringing new life to our small family here. I hope you can be happy for us because it is completely unexpected for us, too."

Colonel Michaels and Dr. Patel, who had been privy to the news for some time, were the only two who did not appear surprised. Everyone else's jaws dropped when they heard the word "pregnant." They all turned to look at Colonel Michaels, expecting him to be as taken aback as they were. His reaction seemed oddly subdued in the face of such a monumental announcement.

The colonel, in an effort to calm everyone down, began, "I know you are looking at me, wondering why I am not stunned. Dr. Patel and I have already been informed. Liz told her about it several days ago, and Arpita informed me this morning. Let's not worry too much right now; I guess congratulations are in order for the parents-to-be."

"Congratulations, guys," said Julien. "I don't want to put a damper on the situation, but I think it's clear that your child will not be able to return home with us 15 years from now."

Colonel Michaels immediately leaned over and whispered in Julien's ear, "Please, Julien. This is not the time for this. Just let them enjoy the moment."

The colonel's warning came too late. Julien's comment startled Liz. She looked toward him and said, "Julien, what do you mean by that? The baby will return home with us; it's pretty obvious. The baby is not an outsider but part of our family, and whatever is part of us will return with us to our time. We were told that. Isn't that right, Colonel?" A look of anger and expectation came over her face.

Liz's question put the colonel in a tough spot. He did not want to answer the question definitively without double-checking. In his heart, he thought Julien was probably right. But he felt it best not to say so at that moment.

The colonel looked to Liz and responded in a conciliatory tone. "The instructions given to us were that anything that was a part of us would return with us to our time. However, I am unsure whether this applies to any children who were conceived and born here. We were never supposed to have children in the first place. Dr. Patel and I will review the medical information that has been sent along with us to find a definite answer."

Colonel Michaels had hoped that this would put everyone at ease, but Julien had opened a pandora's box.

"Colonel, that is absolutely ridiculous," said Willie. Turning toward Liz and in a reassuring tone, he continued, "Our baby will return with us. I'm confident about it."

Colonel Michaels repeated, "I'll research it. I'll check into the computer files. Until then, let's assume the baby will be coming back with us."

The group split up and went off about their own business, each commenting on the unexpected revelation.

Dr. Patel accompanied Willie and Liz into Liz's room to go over *What to Expect When You're Expecting*. Both Liz and Willie were very grateful to Dr. Patel; she seemed as happy as they were about the pregnancy and was enthusiastic about calmly explaining the details of labor and birth. At one time or another, each of the team members commented on how, of all the people in the crew, Dr. Patel always seemed to display a kind and understanding demeanor. Liz felt reassured by having Dr. Patel to guide her through her pregnancy.

Colonel Michaels left the table and went straight to the computers in the laboratory to confirm whether any baby conceived in the future would be able to return with them to the past. Denise, also thinking that any child created here would not be able to return, accompanied the colonel to the computers.

"How do you think Liz became pregnant?" Denise asked the colonel. "I mean, I know she was taking her pills."

With a shrug, the colonel replied, "I intend to ask Dr. Patel that same question. I guess nothing is 100 percent certain. As for now, let's look into the files to see if we can find anything on pregnancies."

Julien and Andrea slipped into the living area to watch a movie. Sitting close to her, Julien remarked, "I have no idea how this all happened. It doesn't make sense, especially when we have been taking the pills every week."

With a devilish grin, Andrea leaned over and replied in a whisper, "The way she kept jumping back and forth between Nicholas's and Willie's beds, maybe the pills weren't powerful enough!"

They both chuckled. Then, becoming serious, Andrea continued, "Maybe, after the shock at the death of Nicholas, her body did not respond to the pills as might be expected. Besides, having a baby around here will certainly cheer things up."

Julien didn't want the conversation to turn somber. He grinned. "Perhaps we should take a cue from Liz and Willie. Why don't you slide over a little closer?"

"Jules, come on, stop it, will you," Andrea responded unconvincingly. Julien had been flirting with her for quite some time, and he was beginning to wear her down. Initially, she tried to resist his advances; her religious upbringing had left her averse to the idea of a casual romance. But now, 9,000 years away from the only world she had ever known, her feelings had begun to change.

She wasn't used to all this male attention, and she had to admit to herself that she was enjoying it immensely. And after all, she told herself, Julien was a really nice guy!

Julien slid even closer to Andrea and took her hand and put it on his lap. She pulled it away, feigning resistance, while looking around and smiling. "Julien, please. Not now. Everyone will be coming in here very soon."

Julien did not seem too interested in the movie or concerned about the others coming in. He leaned toward Andrea and said,

"Come on, baby. Let's not wait till the end of the movie. Let's head to my room!"

Andrea, still a little uncomfortable, replied, "Please, Julien, just relax. Hang on till everyone has gone to bed!"

Both pretended to watch a movie while holding hands discreetly. As soon as everyone else had retreated to their rooms and turned off their lights, the couple turned off the television and disappeared into Julien's room.

The next morning, Colonel Michaels and Denise were up early, still trying to confirm whether or not Liz's baby would return with them. Denise looked at the chronometer.

Chapter 10

The Unthinkable

TIME REMAINING				
YEARS	***DAYS***	***Hours***	***Minutes***	***Seconds***
15	***209***	***20***	***33***	***16***

The effort was mind-boggling. Denise, obviously frustrated, blurted out, "I swear there are like millions of summaries and references on the computer. It's unbelievable. Sometimes, too much information is as bad as too little!"

She then went on to voice what was really bothering her. "Colonel, assuming the worst, what happens if the baby cannot return with us? How can we just let it stay here by itself? There are no humans other than us here."

The colonel was quick to respond, as if he had anticipated the question. "In that case, we would have to do whatever it takes to ensure it is prepared for its survival here after we leave and go back to our time. And I want to remain confident that we will soon find other people."

"The idea of leaving a child alone here is preposterous and monstrous. My mind recoils from such a possibility," Denise responded.

"Hold on, Denise. We still have plenty of time here. This just gives more urgency to our task of finding other people."

Andrea had spent most of the next day scoping out the area and surrounding territories with her drones and capturing as much footage as possible. She then spent hours reviewing the footage but could not find anything worthwhile. There simply was no obvious trace of humans ever being in the area.

Colonel Michaels approached Andrea after dinner. "Andrea, did you find anything interesting in your drone footage today?"

"Colonel Michaels," she sighed, "do you want me to tell you what you want to hear or what I really saw?"

Colonel Michaels knew what was coming next and said, "Lay it on me."

Andrea responded in a discouraged tone, "I will give you one short answer. NOTHING! There is nothing for miles around except beautiful scenery," she sighed again. "So, if you enjoy trees, streams, deer, and crows, it makes for excellent viewing. But I have found no sign of homo-sapiens at all. So far, all the evidence points to the fact that there has been no human life here for at least 1000 years."

Julien overheard their conversation and jokingly chimed in, "I wouldn't be surprised if our race had gone through reverse evolution where we have become ape men."

Andrea smiled and added, "I wish I could see a monkey. It would be something different to look at besides an endless sea of squirrels, rabbits, and chipmunks. If we came here to make a documentary for the National Geographic channel, we'd be in luck."

Denise then joined in on the conversation. "I swear, this is all we see for so many hours every single day. It is a tedious, boring, and tiring exercise. The mind tends to wander, and we might miss something. I think we should all help review some footage every day. Andrea could use a break."

This brought a smile to Andrea's face. "That's a wonderful idea!"

Julien didn't miss the opportunity to impress his girl. "Count me in. I would love to help you two lovely ladies out, I have plenty of time. As you all know, nothing ever breaks down around here and so I am almost always available." He moved in close to Andrea and whispered, "All you have to do is let me know if I can do anything for you."

Andrea put her finger to her lips and whispered, "Shhhh…"

Colonel Michaels addressed them all. "Team, please be patient. We really have only begun our search, and the day we find other people, we'll forget all about how hard it was to stumble upon them."

He then cleared his throat. "We have an announcement for you all. Before we start tonight's movie, I want to update you on our progress. Dr. Hannah – uh, Denise – and I have been scouring the computer for information on the likelihood of Liz's baby returning with us or having to stay here."

Liz's eyes lit up in anticipation of what she expected to be good news.

Colonel Michaels took a deep breath and, as dispassionately as possible, reported what he and Denise had learned.

"After looking through hundreds of reports for the past couple of days, we discovered where this question was asked directly, and answered conclusively, in a comprehensive report prepared by the team of genetic scientists. They stated that all travelers must take pregnancy prevention pills because if any conception occurred, the resulting baby would be unable to return with the travelers."

He took another deep breath and, turning his gaze towards the parents-to-be, adopted a more sympathetic tone. "Liz and Willie, I am sorry to be the bearer of bad news. Your baby will not return with us to our time."

Willie and Liz were stunned. "What?!" Willie exclaimed, "But you have to do something, Colonel. We can't leave our child alone here!"

Liz crossed her hands over her belly and gently rubbed it while insisting, "There are no ifs, ands, or buts. I do not care what you say. It is my baby, and it will be returning to our time with us. I will never leave it here, and it is ridiculous to expect that I will. It is part of Willie and me, and it will come back with us."

She paused briefly, and then went on: "I have a solution. I will not return to our time. I will stay here with my baby."

Willie chimed in, "Our baby!"

Colonel Michaels knew he was treading through a minefield of calamity and tender feelings. "I wish I had something hopeful to say, but I don't. You won't have a choice. None of us has a choice. In 15 years and (looking at the clock) 209 days, we're all going back, and there is nothing we can do about it. We're all going back, and that baby isn't – that's just the way it is."

Liz got up out of the chair crying and went into her room. Willie followed her with a dejected glance at Colonel Michaels. The colonel shook his head in dismay; he was powerless to alter the rules of physics. It was his job to make the tough calls, but this was one time he wished he was not the guy in charge – the guy responsible for breaking such bad news to the young couple.

Sitting on the edge of Liz's bed, the couple embraced and held each other tightly. The baby had given them a common bond stronger than lust or loneliness ever could. And Liz felt that Willie was surely the one man who would do anything for her and her baby. For the first time since she had met him way back during their training days, Liz began to feel real warmth toward Willie.

Colonel Michaels advised everyone to leave Willie and Liz alone for a while to let them come to terms with this harsh reality. He then went on: "Tomorrow, at dinner, we'll come up with a plan of action for the child. It sure would be great if we found some people around here!

"Andrea, Denise and Julien said they would help you review the drone footage. Please don't miss anything. Now that we are done with tonight's business, you may all go back to your rooms unless you want to stay back and see the movie. I think it is time we began to expand our search beyond the fifty-kilometer radius we have been limiting ourselves to. Andrea, plan on you and Julien going out to the end of the drone's range tomorrow, camping out, and sending the drones beyond the limits of what we have surveyed so far."

Chapter 11

Another Mission

TIME REMAINING				
YEARS	***DAYS***	***Hours***	***Minutes***	***Seconds***
15	***152***	***11***	***31***	***58***

Weeks passed. One night, after everyone had completed their duties, the crew gathered around the table for dinner.

Willie turned to Dr. Patel and asked, "Who has cooking duty this week?"

Denise spoke up, "I believe someone else should take over next week, considering the colonel and I have been tasked to prepare the feasts every night for the past seven days, and we're tired of it."

Willie agreed, saying, "I concur! I'm getting a little tired of Colonel Michaels's rabbit enchiladas."

Denise responded without a pause, "The good news is that we will not have to worry about choking down the colonel's rabbit enchiladas any longer!"

"That's the best news I have heard this week," said Willie. "Thank goodness! So, what's on the menu?"

"We are having chicken enchiladas!" smiled Denise.

Willie rolled his eyes and moaned. The crew got settled around the table, and Colonel Michaels began serving the meal. After dinner was done and the dishes cleaned, the colonel asked everyone to remain around the dining room table.

"That was a great meal," he began, "Dr. Patel and I have been working hard with Denise, Andrea, and Julien to figure out how to raise the child here and then keep it safe when we head back. It is crucial to remember that our duty and mission from the very beginning was to discover what happened to humanity.

"Yet we must now recognize that we have two missions. The first mission is to continue our search for people, and now secondly, to prepare this child to survive after we leave it here alone. This year's crops are harvested and soon the weather will be turning colder, and there will be less and less we can do outside. We will devote much of the next few weeks to laying out a plan for developing the sorts of skills anyone would need to survive here – the skills this child will need after we are gone."

Pausing to collect his thoughts, the colonel continued: "The child will be 15 when we leave. But he or she will not have this compound, or all the tools we have brought with us. They will all be gone, returning with us to the past. So, it is for us to learn how to use local resources to make bows and arrows, to sharpen stones for arrowheads, to weave nets for catching fish – all out of local materials. We must find nearby sources of flint to make fires, and learn to gather thatch to build grass huts in which to live. We will do our best to find plants that have medicinal value."

The colonel had laid out what seemed like a superhuman effort.

Julien immediately raised his hand and was given the floor.

"Colonel, perhaps all this is not necessary. Won't there be another mission to the future within a day or so of our return? That's what we were told."

The others nodded in agreement, mumbling "yeah," and "right." Liz and Willie were particularly eager to hear the colonel's response.

Speaking to the team, but directing his gaze to Liz and Willie, the colonel replied, "Does anyone here seriously want to take that for granted? A lot can happen in 16 years, you know. We were told at our final briefing that another mission was being prepared, to be launched and landed 70 or 80 miles from here. But I never heard in what direction. And even if we assume that there will be another mission, we have no idea if those plans might have changed. They might well decide to send it from an entirely different continent for all we know; after all, we haven't had much success in this region so far. And the next mission is unlikely to have the means for intercontinental travel."

"Well," Liz interjected, "we can tell them about the child when we return, and they can change the location of the launch to where we are right now."

"Twenty-four hours would not give them enough time to make such a significant change, Liz," the colonel replied gently. There's simply no guarantee that the child will be found by humans from the next mission! We can hope for the best, but we must be prepared for the worst."

No one on the team tried to argue with the colonel's logic; the wisdom of his words was self-evident. The meeting returned to where it had begun.

Andrea was first to speak up. "If Denise gives me the scientific names of some medicinal plants that might be found in the area, I think I can reprogram the drones to identify them whenever they are spotted. I'm desperate to look for something other than human footprints or abandoned shacks and campsites."

Colonel Michaels stepped in again. "The child will not be ready to learn survival skills for at least six or seven years. This gives the rest of us plenty of time to figure them out for ourselves, master them, and be prepared to teach them.

"As soon as it is feasible, we need to begin trying to live off the land and to catch our own food using only local materials like sharpened stones and home-made traps. We have to live like this child is going to live, so that we can teach it what it will need to know to survive.

"And Willie, let me say that with your love of the outdoors and your inherent ability to bond with nature, you are the best father this child could ask for. I'm sure you will work hard to teach it everything you know about the outdoors and about plants and animals."

Willie seemed assured and responded confidently, "Roger, boss. You know I will."

But all the talk of the child having to survive on its own was too much for Liz. Soon tears were streaming down her face, and she got up and ran into her room.

Alone in his room later that evening, Colonel Michaels contemplated the responsibilities that had been added to their mission as a result of the unanticipated complication. Tomorrow evening, he told himself, he would gather the group around the table and begin working on a list of all the things a person would need to know to survive on their own in what appeared to be a wilderness devoid of other humans. He prayed to God that they would find other people, and that those people would be friendly towards them, rather than either a very primitive or a highly advanced civilization that might fear and be hostile to the newcomers.

The next evening, the team excitedly gathered around the kitchen table. All were reenergized with the new task of developing survival skills. Colonel Michaels began taking notes.

"All right. Let's get this show on the road. If anyone thinks of anything, just blurt it out. I will make a list of the skills we need to develop and practice. I will then go into the computers and find all I can on them. I will print out whatever I find, and we can meet again and decide who is going to tackle what. Then we will devise a timetable for mastering these tasks. So, who has any ideas?"

Willie began, "He will need to be trained in skinning game and tanning leather for clothing."

Liz gave Willie a puzzled look, "You said 'he'? How could you be so sure our baby will be a boy? It could very well be a 'she' you know."

Denise then looked toward Dr. Patel and asked, "Dr. Patel, can you find out whether the baby will be a boy or a girl? This information may be vital to us as we develop its training plans."

Dr. Patel answered, "We do have ultrasound equipment here. I am not an expert at reading ultrasound images. However, in a few months, things should be clear enough for anyone to see. We should know a few months in advance of its birth whether it is a boy or a girl."

"It doesn't matter whether the child is a boy or a girl," Julien remarked. "It will still need to know how to make a fire, build a shelter, hunt, and survive in the elements. Thankfully, the offspring of the animals, like the offspring of humans, will remain here."

Andrea then volunteered, "My drones are sophisticated enough to identify tree species. I can begin mapping out the locations of wild apples and peaches, stands of blackberries, ponds, and streams. An entire map of the flora and fauna of the local area can be made. We can train the child on the locations of all these things."

Colonel Michaels was very excited to see everyone's enthusiastic responses. "That's an excellent idea, Andrea. That will be your primary baby-related assignment. Does anyone else have any ideas to share? All of these suggestions are valuable."

Denise raised her hand. "My mother and I used to sew together when I was a little girl. I remember really enjoying it.

I think I would like to try to put together some baby clothes out of the extra clothing that was sent along with us here."

"You can do it for practice," said Julien. "But remember, we brought all those clothes with us, so they will return with us. For the next 15 years the child will be able to wear anything made from our clothes, but after that, it will have to wear fig leaves or animal skins."

Denise nodded. "We'll have to figure out how to use them for clothes and replace the ones made out of our materials. Willie will be able to provide me plenty of skins, I'm sure."

Willie smiled and said, "I have a lot of them just lying around now. We'll have to learn to tan them. I took a taxidermy class when I was a teenager. I think I can remember how to do it."

All through the day, everyone tossed ideas around. Arguments sometimes developed over things like the possibility of creating pottery or the use of deer bladders to store and carry water. But the crew was excited and reinvigorated by the possibility of accomplishing something so important. Their inability to find any trace of humanity had made every day seem like a pointless failure. But with the baby coming, every member was rejuvenated.

Chapter 12

Unbelievable

TIME REMAINING				
YEARS	***DAYS***	***HOURS***	***MINUTES***	***SECONDS***
15	***58***	***9***	***42***	***51***

The next three months passed quickly as everyone kept busy learning to sew and weave, search for flint, or learn to boil water in an animal bladder. One evening, the crew – minus a couple of members – were seated around the dinner table as usual.

"Where are Julien and Andrea?" Densie asked. "Oh, here they come!"

Andrea and Julien walked in, a worried look on their faces. They didn't sit down, but instead remained standing, waiting for everyone's eyes to turn in their direction. Once they had the room's full attention, Julien spoke up.

"This will probably shock you as much as it has shocked us, but we have a very strong feeling that Andrea is pregnant."

Colonel Michaels's jaw dropped, "What in the hell is going on here? Another pregnancy! Andrea, please tell me this isn't true!"

Andrea then took a long, deep breath and said, "I am afraid to say that I think it is true. We both have taken the pregnancy tablets every week, which is something you have seen us all do! I have no idea how it happened!"

Colonel Michaels, shell-shocked, asked, "And Julien is the father?"

Andrea sighed and said, "Yes, of course, Julien is the father."

The colonel could barely contain his frustration. "This is serious! Having children here was not part of our agenda. This is the second pregnancy, and we haven't even completed a year here!"

The colonel turned to Julien with a look of both disappointment and anger. "We will have to take some drastic steps. What I mean is that we will be cutting things off the men around here! How could the two of you be so foolish? You already knew that this happened with Willie and Liz. We were worried about one child, and now we have to contend with two. You also know that your child will be staying here too. I do not know what to say, honestly. This has made things more complicated."

Julien responded, "It's the pills, the pills. We were shocked, too. Those pills! We took them weekly with the rest of you! I have no idea how or why this happened, but it did. Somehow or other, the potency of those pills must have deteriorated during time travel, or they mutated in some way – heaven only knows how!"

"Something is seriously wrong here," the colonel went on, still fuming. "Whatever happened to those pills, we can rule out their effectiveness as of now." Turning to Dr. Patel, he suggested they skip dinner and go directly to the lab to figure out what was wrong with the pills. "They did not equip this place with a nursery!" he declared in angry frustration.

Dr. Patel and the colonel jumped up and moved promptly into the laboratory to perform some tests on the contraceptive pills.

After a few moments, the colonel turned to the doctor and said, "I feel like I'm becoming an amateur chemist, Arpita. But I do want to tell you that I am glad you have been so wonderful and patient during these trying situations. I sometimes get frustrated with our lack of success in finding any traces of people, and these two pregnancies have got me on edge. You have been a godsend to me. You may not know it, but I lean on you more than all the rest of the crew combined."

Dr. Patel blushed a bit at the colonel's sudden outburst of gratitude and emotion. "You've done a spectacular job leading our group through disappointment and unexpected surprises," Dr. Patel responded, as if to return a compliment. "You and I are not trained chemists. I hope we can figure out what is going on with these pills."

Colonel Michaels replied, "If we do not figure out what is happening here, we will all end up becoming trained babysitters."

Dr. Patel looked up at him, “Thankfully, there is one good thing about this.”

“Please enlighten me, Doctor,” said the colonel. “Whatever is good about this situation, I’d like to know what it is.”

“Well, I love babies, and I’ve always wanted to have children of my own,” she replied.

“Oh my God, not you too, Arpita!” exclaimed the colonel. I hope these two couples have not encouraged you to try to join their parade! We have enough clowns in this circus!”

“Ha, ha, ha. You crack me up, my colonel. I love babies, but I am not able to have children. You won’t have to worry about that. I do not need the pregnancy pills either. Years ago, when I was much younger, I got pregnant, and there were serious difficulties. I had a little girl, but she died in childbirth after severe complications. It left me unable to have more children, but that didn’t change my love for them.”

She stared off into the distance. “My child was a beautiful baby girl. I named her Jahnvi. My little Jahnvi,” she murmured.

Colonel Michaels was sorry for Dr. Arpita Patel’s loss. He had never had any children himself, but he imagined that losing a child would be the hardest thing for any expecting mother. Dr. Patel was obviously fighting back tears as she recounted the story.

The colonel was not an overly emotional man, but he was compassionate. The team had become his family, maybe even something like his children, and he wanted to be their leader in any crisis and their guardian during any peril. He struggled to be their go-to-person for any and every concern. But he noted that, as often as not, team members preferred to share their troubles with Dr. Patel. He didn't see her as a competitor, but as a great help in leading his crew.

Dr. Patel looked back at her computer screen and was taken aback. It was as if a light bulb in her head had suddenly clicked on.

"Colonel Michaels, take a look here, please. I think I have figured out the cause of our conundrum."

Colonel Michaels looked at the screen, "What is it? I can't figure out what you are looking at."

"There are no hormones or enzymes in these pills at all. Not even many vitamins. Apparently, we have all been taking only very low-dose vitamins and expecting them to prevent pregnancy. Ha!"

"That's terrible! What are we going to do now?" fretted the colonel. "Can you do something, Arpita? I mean, can you concoct something that can serve as birth control? After all, we still have to remain here for many, many years. I don't understand how such a mistake could have been made!"

Dr. Patel sighed and said, "Colonel, I am very tired now. I don't believe they sent along anything that would work as a contraceptive. I mean, they thought they did send something, so there would have been no reason to send anything additional along those lines. But I'll begin looking into it tomorrow."

Colonel Michaels could not believe what he had just been told. He had no clue how or why such a monumental blunder could have occurred. He knew he had to break the news to the rest of the crew.

The next morning at breakfast, while everyone was still at the table, Colonel Michaels briefed everyone.

"Dr. Patel has discovered that the contraceptive pills we were provided are nothing more than plain vitamins. This explains the pregnancies. I assume this was a terrible mistake. What it means for us is that we must be doubly careful. You all must be doubly careful. Please sleep in your own beds; I cannot stress this enough!"

Everyone looked at each other with astonishment. Dr. Patel spoke up, "I understand this is a bit hard to swallow, but relax. Liz and Andrea are both pregnant, so there is nothing to worry about with them for a while. However, once their babies are born, they will both be capable of getting pregnant again. We must not allow this to happen! The colonel and I cannot prevent this; only you can."

Later that evening, Colonel Michaels found Dr. Patel in the medical laboratory looking over medical reports and the inventory of drugs she had been provided.

He came up behind her and said, "Why don't you give it a rest until tomorrow. Everyone is gathered in front of the television watching a funny movie. Why don't you join us?"

The doctor felt grateful for the colonel's concern. She could tell that he had the welfare of each individual crew member on his mind, even hers.

She smiled and replied, “Colonel, I have admired your leadership skills over the past few months. I am amazed at how well you’ve handled all our crises, big and small; and you deal so well with the various personalities on our team. I’ve often wondered if this was due to your training or if you are just a natural leader.”

“Well,” the colonel began, “you are all technical specialists. I was sent along as a generalist. I often reflect on your great skills, and the abilities of the others, and I wonder what it is that I have to offer. If I can lend a bit of support to each member of the crew in some personal way, I feel like I am contributing, and doing my part to help out.”

The doctor had no idea Colonel Michaels was so introspective. He had never opened up like this to her before – just as she had never opened up to him before she shared the story of the loss of her child. It was clear that an emotional bond was developing as each took comfort in the other’s company.

Chapter 13

Success at Last!

TIME REMAINING				
YEARS	***DAYS***	***Hours***	***Minutes***	***Seconds***
15	***35***	***7***	***51***	***32***

The weeks passed and Liz and Andrea both grew rounder. The time was getting close for Liz to have her baby, and Andrea was going to have her child just a few months afterwards. Everyone began what seemed like a monumental task, of trying to master the crafts of carving arrowheads and making spear points, all the while looking for signs of what happened to human civilization.

The two unexpected pregnancies had put a new complexion on the relationships among the crew. Everyone seemed to have become one big family. Denise had taken over a lot of the duties formerly done by Liz and Andrea, who seemed to need a lot of rest now. She routinely ventured out for miles with one of the men, navigating Andrea's drones for her, and still looking for signs of human civilization.

When not attending to the drones, Denise was usually seen sitting on the ground, trying to mold a pot out of clay or push a sharpened bone through a tough hide. The latter endeavor usually ended with her swearing and cursing when the bone broke. More than once, she threw both the bone and hides to the ground, cussing, while storming into the compound yelling something like, "*How the hell am I supposed to sew skins together with a sharpened bone!? This is impossible!*"

The only break she got was when she was out on "drone duty" in the field with one of the men. The switch from exhausting and frustrating hard work to sitting around looking at endless images of trees and grass was a welcome respite. "My fingers get time to heal and recuperate when I'm out here," Denise was heard to say more than once.

One sunny day, while in the woods, miles from the main compound, Denise and Julien were loafing in front of their tents, getting glassy eyed watching the endless hours of video signals the drones were sending back in real time. The drones had been programmed to beep and send an alert signal every time a suspiciously symmetrical structure was scanned. Suddenly, one of the drones sent back an alert. Denise perked up.

"Hey Julien," she exclaimed loudly, "This drone is sending an alert now!"

Julien rushed to look over Denise's shoulder at the screen. "Does that look like something to you?" he asked, as he stared into the screen.

"It sure does," she replied excitedly.

They couldn't believe their eyes. They stood there stunned as they gazed upon what appeared to be the foundation of a building. "At last, at last!" Denise shouted with unreserved excitement. They looked at each other for a second, and then jumped into each other's arms, laughing. Julien actually picked Denise up and swung her around and around.

"We've waited all these months to find something, and at last we have!" Denise shouted, as if Julien hadn't realized the magnitude of their discovery. "Andrea is going to be so mad that I found it without her," she laughed.

"Hey, don't forget about me," Julien teased. "I was here helping, you know."

"Oh yeah," laughed Denise, "I couldn't have done it without you." She went on sarcastically. "You were protecting me from lions and tigers and bears, while I was busy finding humanity. I'll agree to share a small amount of the glory with you to the news reporters when we get home."

She sent the command for the drone to get as low to the structure as possible. But it was surrounded by tall trees and brush. She looked at Julien and told him, "The drone can't get very low. It's too cluttered there. But I can have it hover over the site. The drone is located only about 4 miles northwest of us. We can travel there in our four-wheeler."

Julien noticed that the terrain looked pretty rough in that direction. "It may be only four miles from here, but it won't be easy getting there," he warned.

They both jumped into the four-wheeler and headed for the spot where the drone was hovering. They were giddy with anticipation and couldn't help reaching out and grabbing each other's hand every few minutes as they traveled. The vehicle had to move at a frustratingly slow speed over the rough and tree-filled terrain.

Finally, as they approached the site, Denise spotted the drone hovering only about 300 feet in front of them. "Stop, stop" she yelled. "There's the drone."

The four-wheeler hadn't even come to a complete stop when she jumped out and pushed her way through the undergrowth to find what the drone had spotted. She held a trowel in her hand as she expected to be digging through the ruins any minute.

Julien caught up with her and said, "Whoa, slow down! This thing has been here for years, probably centuries; it's not going anywhere now."

She laughed and said, "Finally, I'm going to earn my pay as the crew's archeologist on this trip. It will certainly be the most important dig I have ever been on."

As they approached the spot, they climbed onto a rock outcropping to look down at what the drone had discovered. Both stood in stunned silence. It was a rectangular symmetrical structure all right. But upon close examination, it was clear that it was just another rock formation that was coincidentally rectangular in shape. The drone was simply unable to get close enough to show them on the screen that it was not worth their time to investigate.

Denise seemed more than dejected. Coming down from such a high almost brought tears to her eyes. Julien could see that she was far more emotionally upset about their disappointment than he was. He put his arm around her and said, "Hey, don't give up. This might be a good sign of things to come."

But Denise was no fool. She realized that they had been searching for months without discovering even the slightest clue of what might have happened to the human race.

"It's getting dark," said Julien. "Let's go back to the tents and tell each other some funny stories. I know a few jokes sure to make you laugh."

Denise gave Julien a half-smile. They locked their arms as they made their way back to the four-wheeler and then back to their tents.

The next day, they packed up and returned to the compound. Denise was disappointed but felt a new bond with Julien over the incident. She could see how Andrea could fall for such a nice guy.

That night at dinner, Denise told the group about the amazing discovery that "almost was." The rest of the group were on the edges of their seats as they listened to Denise's adventure, and all showed their disappointment when she got to the end and had to reveal that it was just another false alarm.

Denise and Julien had been out for days and were anxious to crawl into a real bed and get a good night's sleep. Liz's and Andrea's pregnancies sapped their strength, and both retired early to bed. Willie, never far from Liz's side, joined her. This left the colonel and Dr. Patel alone at the kitchen table.

The two had made it a habit of staying up later than the others. Sometimes they'd just talk about their past, or of what the future might have in store for them when they returned back. Some nights they'd play gin, and other nights cribbage. The colonel loved to play cards and he brought along 200 decks as part of his personal weight allowance. Never having had a family, he had to occupy his hours and days in other pursuits. One of them was card playing at the officer's club, which he tried to do as often as possible.

He seemed anxious to show Arpita how to play all of the games he enjoyed. She was not much of a card player but being alone with the colonel night after night had become a very pleasant routine for her. She felt closest to him while playing cards. It was a favorite activity that only they shared. He seemed most at ease and at his most relaxed when playing cards alone with her.

"The thing I miss the most," began the colonel, "is a good cigar. I used to smoke one almost every night, on my front porch, while looking at the stars. The sky here is much darker. I can see so many more stars here. I wanted to give them up, so I didn't bring any along on this trip. I didn't realize how much I'd miss them."

Arpita pinched her nose with her fingers. "Those things stink. India just passed a law prohibiting the sale or use of tobacco. But I have smelled them in your country and in Europe. I'm glad you didn't bring any along. It is good karma for you, sparing the rest of us the smell."

"Well, what is your weakness, my good doctor? Or don't you have any flaws?" the colonel asked with a smile.

"My passion is for hard candy!" The doctor responded enthusiastically. "I brought along ten pounds of assorted hard candies, but I've eaten almost half of them already. My favorite is butterscotch."

"Umm butterscotch" the colonel agreed.

The following evening, while playing their nightly game of cribbage, it became apparent that the colonel had something on his mind. He made a few unusual and foolish mistakes in the card game and Dr. Patel finally looked at him and said, "Colonel, are you trying to let me win this game?"

The colonel laughed a little, paused, looked at the doctor, and said, "It's easy to see how those young people become involved. I mean, just by being around each other, it is natural that they would be drawn together. And I must say, and I sincerely mean it, that you are also a very attractive woman."

Dr. Patel looked at him and smiled, "Thanks for noticing! But it's your turn to deal."

She tried to act as if the colonel's words had no effect on her, but in fact, the compliment was as welcome as it was unexpected. There was clearly chemistry between the two senior members of the group. However, Colonel Micheals had been determined to keep all relationships professional. And, as if by instinct, both knew what the other was thinking. He cleared his throat a bit and said, "You and I have to set an example for the others in matters of personal relationships. Otherwise, we will lose focus on the mission."

Dr. Patel rolled her eyes and said, "I believe the crew is setting an example for us, my card playing friend."

Colonel Michaels looked puzzled. "What do you mean?"

"You are an admirable leader, but I am sorry to have to point out that you have one shortcoming."

"And what is that, Arpita?" Colonel Michels smirked and asked.

"I feel that you are very slow in one particular area, very slow indeed," she replied.

"What are you talking about?" he repeated.

Dr Patel smiled, leaned over the cribbage board and gave him a light kiss on his lips, thinking to herself, "If I don't make some sort of move, we may be stuck just playing card games for the next 15 years."

"I hope I have transmitted my message clearly enough for even someone as slow as you to understand," smiled Arpita. "At least for us, we don't have to worry about pregnancies and babies!"

Colonel Michaels was happily taken aback, being unprepared for her bold assertion. He had long harbored feelings for the kind doctor but was careful to keep them to himself. He had wondered if her emotions were leading her in the same direction, but he never mustered up the courage to test them. Now things were different.

He walked over to look down the hall to make sure that everyone was already in bed. Then he looked at the doctor and said, "I think I'll need you to come to my room to retransmit that message."

She smiled and said, "I suppose you're conceding this game to me then, eh? But you come to my room. Give me a few minutes first; I will leave the door unlocked."

Colonel Michaels was puzzled. "I'm not sure what difference it makes, your room or my room?"

Dr. Patel smiled and said, "I have seen your room. It is a little too messy. I suspect it might smell in there too. So…."

Colonel Michaels spoke up indignantly, "Come on, Arpita, it does not smell in there – I don't think? Anyway, how did you see my room? You do know that we are not supposed to enter anyone else's personal area without an invitation."

Dr. Patel chuckled and said, "I have been in the hallway a couple of times when you opened the door to your room. You are very impressive in several ways. However, housecleaning is not one of them."

Early the next morning, Andrea was up before everyone else, making coffee, as had become her routine. She heard something and looked down the hallway just in time to see the colonel sneaking out of Dr. Patel's room. She quickly ducked so he didn't see her.

Andrea couldn't wait to break the news to the rest of her crewmates in the morning. As Julien walked into the kitchen, she excitedly revealed her discovery. "Hey Julien, guess what I saw this morning? Colonel Michaels creeping out of Dr. Patel's room!" Julien smiled and responded, "I was wondering if the old boy had any red blood cells left. I guess all this sex lecturing has got his mind focused on the problem. Of course, he didn't know how happy he was without a woman. Now it's too late. Poor bastard."

"You're a jerk!" Andrea quipped. They were both laughing when Denise walked in and asked, "What's so funny?"

Andrea couldn't hold back her excitement. "Guess what I just saw?"

Julien smirked, winked at Andrea, and said, "Let me give her a clue; it involves Colonel Michaels and Dr. Patel."

Denise began to laugh too, saying, "Wow! That's so interesting. Do you think they're a thing? I just saw him carrying a bucket of soapy water into his room and he told me he was going to give it a good cleaning. He also told me not to be afraid to tell anyone about it. How weird!"

Ten days later, Liz finally went into labor. She gave birth to a little boy whom she named Liam, after Willie's father and grandfather. Everyone looked at the clock at the very moment the baby was born so that they would notice and record that this was exactly how old the little boy would be when everyone returned to the past and he was left here.

Chapter 14

Babies!

TIME REMAINING				
YEARS	*DAYS*	*Hours*	*Minutes*	*Seconds*
15	*9*	*10*	*44*	*42*

The first baby was born, and another was on its way. This was a dramatic change for the team and the new baby added color and excitement to their lives. A year had passed and so much had happened.

Four months after the birth of Liam the second new member of their expanding family arrived.

At four months old, Liz's baby was a handsome, blonde haired blue-eyed bundle of joy that everyone treated like a king.

As Andrea went into labor, she was surrounded by the other women anxious to help Arpita with the delivery.

With Liam sleeping soundly, Willie, Julien, and the colonel waited in the kitchen drinking coffee. Colonel Michaels noted that both fathers seemed as happy as he had ever seen them.

Julien spoke up, taking their attention away from the impending moment. "I completed my monthly inventory of provisions yesterday. We were sent about a year's supply of coffee, and that's almost gone. We're going to have to learn to live without it."

Suddenly, they heard the cries of a newborn. The three men instinctively looked up at the clock, noting how old the child would be when they would have to leave it behind.

TIME REMAINING				
YEARS	***DAYS***	***Hours***	***Minutes***	***Seconds***
14	***247***	***15***	***22***	***36***

The next morning, Andrea and Julien were sitting together with their newborn. She couldn't take her eyes off of it as it slept in her arms. She leaned into Julien and whispered softly, "I think she looks like both of us."

Julien smiled. "Yes, she is beautiful. Hey, I want to ask you something. A few months back, after Dr. Patel looked at the ultrasound image and told us that we were having a baby girl, you told me that you wanted to name her Kristina. I didn't give it much thought at the time, but I've been wondering, where did you come up with the name 'Kristina'?"

Andrea's brow furrowed. "Why? Don't you like the name?"

“Of course, I do!” answered Julien. “I was just curious how you came up with it.”

“Didn’t I tell you this already? When I was a little girl, I loved to play with dolls, and my two favorites were Christopher and Kristina. And when I found out that I was pregnant, I knew I was going to name the baby either Kristina or Christopher.”

“Why were you so captivated with those names?” Julien wondered.

“Well, I know religion doesn’t mean much to you, but it means a whole lot to me. I want our baby to grow up believing in something. People need something to believe in, and that name is grounded in my faith. “Kristina” is a girl’s name derived from the name ‘Christ.’ The Bible has comforted me a lot on this trip, and I want our child to know something about it.”

“I should have guessed that was the reason,” Julien confessed.

He went on: “You know that I was raised as a Muslim, but a non-practicing one. I guess it never occurred to my parents to name me Mohammed.”

“You’ve never spoken much about your parents,” Andrea remarked.

“My mother was from Algeria and moved to France as a little girl,” explained Julien. “My father is a civil rights attorney in America. They met in Paris when my father was on vacation there. Both my parents ended up working for NASA at one time or another for different reasons, and I ended up with dual citizenship between the U.S.A. and France. My mom and dad are pretty devout Muslims, but they never forced religion on me, and I can't say I know much about Islam or any other religion. I never considered myself much of a believer in anything. Besides, I thought your dad was a communist. Aren't they all supposed to be atheists?"

"My dad was a communist, and he said he was an atheist too. I know I told you all this before. You just don't listen to me!" replied Andrea, a bit perturbed.

"Well, tell me again," Julien asked.

Andrea rolled her eyes at having to repeat the same things she had told Julien a number of times.

"He met my mom in Beijing when she was working on an article. She was a journalist. And she was a rather devout Christian. He is a genius non-believer, and she is a genius believer. So, I got the best of both worlds. He used to tease her about the Bible when she would sit and read me its stories as a little girl. He didn't believe, but I think he actually admired her for the strength of her conviction. They sent me to America to study, so when it came time for China to participate in this project, I was highly recommended."

"I have a feeling he admired your mother for more than just her religious devotion. Did she have a cute butt?" Julien inquired playfully.

Andrea rolled her eyes again and was clearly not amused by his sense of humor. In her mind, it seemed like he was not really listening to her again, and not taking her devotion to her faith seriously. She was clearly very proud of her beliefs and her parents.

"Listen!" said Andrea in a serious tone, "I always admired my mother's religious devotion, and I think it helped her too. She died of breast cancer when I was only twenty. And the Bible helped her in her final days. I used to sit by her hospital bed and read it to her, just like she used to read it to me when I was small. My dad would come in when I was reading sometimes, and he would never interrupt us. I want our baby to know we are good people, too. And I want her to feel that we are decent, and to respect us like I loved and respected my parents."

"Don't get yourself agitated," said Julien. "I'm fine with the name and I'm fine with our child knowing the Bible. Just don't turn into a religious nut on me. I'm sure we'll be good parents. We'll share the child-rearing responsibilities. You can do most of the work, and I'll try to get most of the credit. Fair enough?" Andrea was hardly paying attention to Julien; her focus was on their baby. She looked down passionately at her newborn and said, "The only thing that I'm going to go nuts over is this baby. This is the best thing that has ever happened to me."

Months passed and Liam and Kristina were growing fast. It seemed like no time at all before little Liam's birthday came around and he was a year old and walking like a champ. Kristina, at eight months, was pulling herself up and looked like she'd be walking soon. Baby formula was not provided in the crew's supplies, and the team seemed to take particular joy in pureeing meats and vegetables, concocting what they believed would be a balanced diet for the babies.

Diapers were not supplied either, but the women made them from the extra clothes that were sent along. Luckily, both mothers were able to breastfeed, and there were plenty of extra clothes to be cut and sewn into children's things. Denise became the head seamstress, and clearly enjoyed helping Liz and Andrea make miniature shirts and pants. Dr. Patel had the final word in all baby food recipes, and together the four women seemed to have formed a professional baby-making and raising squad.

The men checked on the moms and the babies every morning before heading outside. The guys took on a somewhat chauvinistic attitude toward the women and children, beating their chests that they were real men, protecting the group, hunting for food, and weaving nets and traps. The guys always feigned how tired they were when they came inside, when in reality, they were scared to death about being asked to watch the babies when they were so small. At one time or another, each of the men said something to the effect that they would rather wrestle alligators than be asked to change diapers.

At first the girls thought the boys were just jerks. But they soon realized that taking care of diapers and baby baths was a far more pleasant duty then disemboweling sheep and stringing out their intestines to make bow-and-arrow strings – an activity that seemed to occupy the men for hours. A division of labor soon formed. The male world was largely outdoors, dirty and smelly; and the world of the women and children was generally indoors and much safer and cleaner. Both sides seemed satisfied with the arrangement. Denise was the only member who seemed equally at home in both worlds. She was happy making baby clothes and didn't complain when she was outside, working on some project shoulder-to-shoulder with the guys.

With both moms preoccupied with their babies, it had become necessary to realign some of the chores and duties. The two mothers ended up being responsible for cooking most of the meals and cleaning up the common areas. Dr. Patel seemed to be needed to patch up some little scrape or bruise every day on one or another of the guys. On more than a few occasions, she needed to put a stitch or two in the hands of one of the men as they tried again and again to master the art of sharpening flint into cutting tools and spear points.

With Andrea unable to leave her little one for extended periods of time and unable to take her out over long distances in a four-wheeler, Denise assumed most of the long-distance drone surveying. The search had been extended farther and farther away from the compound, but with no more success than before.

Denise ended up leaving for two or three days a week with either the colonel, Julien, or Willie, searching more distant areas, and then they would come back to the compound for a week to double-check the footage with Andrea. However, no matter in which direction they looked, no traces of people had been discovered.

Chapter 15

Nature Will Take Its Course

TIME REMAINING				
YEARS	***DAYS***	***Hours***	***Minutes***	***Seconds***
13	*182*	*8*	*42*	*25*

Six months later, everyone had fallen into a routine. Dr. Patel, Liz, and Andrea stayed home with the kids, cooking most of the meals, cleaning the living areas, and sewing the children's clothes as needed.

The men largely stayed outdoors to work and hunt, except when they were eating or sleeping. The group was beginning to take the job of carving arrowheads and knife blades seriously. Starting a fire with a flint was still the most challenging job. But no matter what was going on at the compound, the colonel continued to pressure them to take the drones farther and farther out to look for signs of civilization. He and Denise were keeping their minds and their focus on their mission, while everyone else was acting as if raising the kids and hunting and fishing were the real purpose of their existence now.

The colonel kept reminding everyone that taking the drones afield was a mission priority. Denise and Julien ended up being the two who were sent out the most. Willie had to tend to the garden, which needed daily oversight. The wild rabbits, skunks, foxes, voles, moles, and chipmunks seemed to consider it their smorgasbord; and weeds were a constant problem. Colonel Michaels suffered from terrible back pain from spending nights in a sleeping bag, and dreaded camping outdoors. And everyone thought it best that Dr. Patel stayed where the children were, in case of accidents.

Consequently, over the past few months, Julien and Denise were carrying out 75 percent of the reconnaissance. They didn't seem to mind. The children had plenty of mothering between Liz, Andrea, and Dr. Patel, and when there was no clothing to fix, Denise was often left with little to do. Accompanying Julien seemed like the most productive way she could occupy her time and contribute to the mission.

The two came to enjoy heading out and surveying together. At the compound, everything revolved around the babies and working on making primitive tools. It came to feel like, if someone wasn't trying to sharpen a rock, then they were goofing off and letting the others down.

The two found that being alone in the woods was peaceful. And with so many hours on their hands, telling each other every detail about their lives became the thing to do. They could feel each other being drawn together, and neither seemed to want to do anything to prevent it. Julien loved Denise's free-spirited attitude, and she learned to tolerate his silly jokes.

"Did you ever wonder what ghosts do when they're just sitting around and not haunting people?" Julien asked, pretending to be serious. Denise laughed and said, "They probably chat about their former lives like we've been doing."

Denise was unaccustomed to the pleasure of having someone to open up to and share her thoughts with. She had always been somewhat of a loner. Her acquaintances were her co-workers. Julien was an uncommonly good listener and seemed genuinely fascinated by her out-of-the-ordinary interests and odd-ball observations.

"I've always had a thing for trees," Denise told him.

"Trees? What's so fascinating about trees?" he asked, as he glanced at the forest that surrounded them.

"Well, you know trees evolved over 200 million years ago along with the dinosaurs. As land animals evolved to enormous proportions, so did the plants. The dinosaurs increased in size to be over 100 feet long and stood three stories tall. Ancient plants followed suit and grew to over 100 feet tall too."

"That's true," Julien nodded.

"Then," continued Denise, "they think an asteroid hit earth about 66 million years ago that wiped out all the dinosaurs. All that was left were smaller creatures. But the asteroid didn't wipe out the trees. Imagine if it had."

"What do you mean?" Julien asked.

Denise's eyes widened as she spoke with some excitement: "Imagine if the trees had gone extinct with the dinosaurs, and all that existed now were grasses and small bushes that grew to only about eight feet tall. What if that was all we had ever known?"

She went on: "And imagine if we were told by scientists that long ago plants had grown to enormous proportions 100, 200, or even 300 feet tall. Dinosaur-plants, you might say. And if we had never seen anything like them, would we even be able to visualize what a world of giant 100-foot-tall plants would look like?"

"Probably not" said Julien, "I guess we'd likely never be able to really conjure up how a world of giant trees would appear -- if we had never experienced it."

"We live in a world of dinosaur-plants," smiled Denise. "And we take them for granted. Huge plants that grow hundreds of feet up into the air, and we never give them a second thought. But things might not have happened as they did. Trees might have gone extinct, along with the dinosaurs. And we'd never have known what it would be like to live alongside giant plants that tower into the sky."

Julien leaned toward her, "I love the term, dinosaur-plants!

I've never heard trees described that way. Did you invent that phrase?"

Denise shrugged as they both gazed up at the canopy that surrounded them.

"I'll probably never be able to look at trees the same way again," Julien remarked.

The more she talked, the more captivated Julien became by the way her mind worked. He enjoyed listening to all her unusual and off-the-wall observations. Time spent alone with Denise was never dull.

"Beauty and brains too. That's an attractive combination," Julien thought to himself.

"Let me ask you a question," Julien ventured. "If you could be only one or the other, would you rather be beautiful or brilliant?"

Denise paused for a moment and then affirmed with a laugh, "I'd want to be both of course. But if I couldn't be both at the same time … I think I'd rather be beautiful now but be remembered as brilliant."

It wasn't long before the two were sharing a tent and exploring all the pleasures that youth, health, and solitude had to offer.

Both of them loved Andrea and didn't really feel like they were betraying her. It was a fling, and nothing more. Whenever they returned to the compound, Julien sat next to Andrea at dinner, and they affectionately referred to each other as mommy and daddy. Denise loved them both, and the last thing she wanted to do was get between them.

Willie, the colonel, Dr. Patel, and Liz always tried to beg off going into the woods to send out the drones. So, it was easy for Julien and Denise to pretend to be put upon, and say, in a reluctant tone, "OK, I guess we'll go out again."

Both knew of the dangers of pregnancy. And both did all they could to avoid it. There were no condoms available, so they just had to be careful on the dates. But nothing is perfect, and it wasn't long before Denise missed her period. She also began feeling nauseous at random times of the day. She knew what that meant, and she wasn't happy about it.

She wasn't one of those little girls who grew up playing "princess" and dreaming of Prince Charming coming along to sweep her off her feet. She loved playing in the dirt and excelling at school. She was headstrong and career oriented, which likely explains why she had never had a serious relationship that lasted for more than a few months. And, not having a long-term relationship, getting married or having kids never seemed to be on the agenda. She volunteered for the mission knowing that it meant she would never have children, and she was fine with that.

Back at the compound, as soon as she saw Julien alone, she pulled him aside and told him the news. He seemed stunned, but somehow not surprised. She told him that she was going to ask Dr. Patel to perform an abortion and keep the fact a secret. Getting pregnant, in spite of their best efforts to avoid it, meant that their little backwoods romance was going to have to come to an end. Julien nodded and didn't say anything more. He seemed too dazed to speak. And he knew he didn't want that sort of trauma to upset everything.

Later that afternoon, Denise found Dr. Patel outside playing with the children while Liz and Andrea were inside preparing the evening meal.

"Hey, Dr. Patel," waived Denise as she approached. "I see you've been put on babysitting duty again."

Dr. Patel looked up and smiled, "These two precious things are no trouble at all. I'd watch them all day but chasing them up and down this hill tires me out."

Denise sat down on the ground next to the doctor, and her tone turned serious. "Doctor, I've got something important to tell you, and I want you to promise me that it will go no farther than between you and me. You know, doctor-patient privilege, and all that."

Dr. Patel's brow furrowed, "What's wrong?"

"Well … I'm pregnant." Denise said matter-of-factly. "I don't want to hurt Andrea, and I am not interested in being a mother."

Dr. Patel interrupted, "Does the father know?"

"Yes, he knows," replied Denise. "And he knows that I'm coming to you to get an abortion. In secret. We'll pretend I have some other female issues, and you need to do some procedure, and it will all be over. No one will ask about details."

Doctor Patel looked at little Liam and little Kristina as they laughed and played, and she shook her head a little.

"Denise," the doctor began, "this is a serious situation. You are carrying a baby. You know how easy it is to love a baby. Everyone knows you love these babies just like their mothers. Are you sure you want to do such a dramatic thing?"

Denise looked determined. "Yes, I've given it a lot of thought and I know the sooner the procedure is performed, the better."

Doctor Patel looked her in the eyes and said, "You know, abortions can be dangerous. I've never done one and have no training in that area."

Denise's voice got firmer, "Do you think I want to face Andrea and tell her that I've been in the woods having sex with Julien? I don't want to cause a problem between them. She would be humiliated."

Dr. Patel replied in a soft voice, "I'm sure she'd be surprised and hurt at first, but we all love each other here."

Densie paused, and then said, "I've given this a lot of thought. I resigned myself to never having children, and I'm alright with that. And now, under these circumstances, I am doubly convinced that an abortion is the right thing to do."

Dr. Patel's eyes darted back and forth between the children and Denise. She knew she was going to refuse to perform the abortion, but she didn't want to confront her directly that way. She was hoping she could persuade Denise to change her mind.

"Look Denise," said the doctor, "I don't want you to think I am lecturing you. But I want you to sleep on this decision tonight. One more day won't make any difference. Look at these beautiful babies. Your baby will be just as beautiful, and just as loved by Andrea and everyone else. Please sleep on it and we'll talk about it tomorrow."

Trying to manipulate Denise into changing her mind, the doctor told her that she was tired and wanted to take a short nap. She asked Denise if she'd stay out here with the kids until supper time. She was hoping in her heart that watching these kids while thinking of her own pregnancy would convince Denise to change her mind and want to have the baby.

A short time later, they were called in to eat. Denise's stomach was in knots as it had been all day. As she sat at the table, it seemed odd that Julien was just sitting there next to Andrea, laughing with the guys, as if nothing at all had changed – as if this did not impact him in the least.

Denise appeared uncomfortable. She was not eating, and she remained very quiet. Colonel Michaels looked at her and asked,

"Was the weather rough out there last week for you and Julien?"

"No," replied Denise, "the weather was fine."

She kept looking over at Dr. Patel, who seemed just as preoccupied with her thoughts as she was. That night, after everyone went to bed, Denise lay awake thinking of her decision.

She loved Liz's and Andrea's kids. But she never wanted one of her own. She knew the doctor hadn't performed the procedure before, but she didn't think it was dangerous. She imagined this was going to have to be the end of her little fling with Julien. She didn't want to go through this scare again. These thoughts kept going around and around in her head until she finally fell asleep.

The next morning, she brushed her teeth and combed her hair and came to the firm conclusion that she wanted the abortion. She heard the others gathering for breakfast and came out of her room to sit with them.

"Where's Dr. Patel?" she asked.

"I encountered her walking through the vegetable garden this morning," replied Willy. "I asked her where she was going, and she said she wanted to take a walk. I asked her if she wanted me to go with her, and she said no. She seemed to want to be alone with her thoughts."

The colonel was standing at the stove, frying up some ham and eggs. Willie was a top-notch farmer, and his chickens produced more eggs than the group could eat; and his pig pens were overrun with piglets. He and Julien had built a smoke house where they cured meats, and both seemed proud of their abilities as outdoorsmen.

"Do you want some ham and eggs, Denise?" the colonel asked.

Just the smell of them was making her nauseous. But she didn't want to make the others suspicious. "No thank you, I'm not hungry this morning," she replied.

Just as everyone was finishing up, Dr. Patel came in from her walk. Denise immediately jumped up and asked to speak with her.

Both women walked back to Dr. Patel's room and closed the door.

“I’ve decided to go through with the abortion,” Denise stated in a business-like manner.

“That’s unfortunate,” replied Dr, Patel, “because I will not perform it.”

“What do you mean?” asked Denise, confused. The idea that the doctor might refuse had never entered her mind.

“Just what I said,” Dr. Patel replied in a firm tone, a tone Denise had never heard the doctor use before.

“This is absurd,” responded Denise, her voice raised. “You are the medical professional sent on this mission to take care of our medical needs. You must do it.”

“Pregnancy is not an illness that you need to be cured of,” said the doctor. “You have to resign yourself to the fact that you are going to have a baby. We will all be here for you and your child. That is what’s best and that is what’s right.”

“Who are you to tell me what is right for me?” Denise demanded, her voice growing loud enough that the others still sitting around the table could hear. “I’ll tell the colonel, and he’ll order you to do it!”

Dr. Patel shook her head. “The colonel and I have already discussed such matters. He knows I will not do it even if ordered to do so.”

“But this is my right,” stated Denise self-assuredly. “This is my body, and I have a right to decide what happens with it.”

Dr. Patel responded, "I have a right to my body as well, and I can't be made to do what I refuse to do. Doesn't my right to my body count as much as your right to yours?"

"This is bullshit!" yelled Denise as she stormed out of the room, charging into her bedroom and slamming the door.

After a few minutes, Dr. Patel joined the others at the breakfast table. "If you don't mind me asking," said the colonel, "what the hell is going on?"

"She'll have to tell you herself," answered the doctor.

Everyone sat there in silence, not knowing what kind of problem could cause a rift between Dr. Patel and Denise. Julien was wishing he could be anywhere but there at that moment.

Denise sat in her room fuming. She had always been the first to compliment Dr. Patel for attending to the crews' fevers, coughs, rashes, and chills. But she couldn't understand this.

She was angry at Dr. Patel and angry that Julien couldn't be of more help. After all, this was his problem too. Irate and resentful, she stormed into the dining area and blurted out, "I'm pregnant. I want to have an abortion. I think that would be best and I think it's my right. Dr. Patel says she will not perform one. I hope we can convince her that she is wrong in this matter."

Everyone was staggered by the announcement, and they had no idea how to respond. Silence fell over the table for several seconds.

Colonel Michaels spoke up, his voice booming. "This is unacceptable! Are you people trying to create more problems for us? Who is the father?"

Liz chimed in, "Who do you think?"

Dr. Patel stared blankly at Colonel Michaels, also asking,

"Who do you think?"

The colonel responded sternly, shaking his head, "I don't know! If I knew, I wouldn't have to ask."

Liz and Dr. Patel both pointed toward Julien and called out his name in unison.

Dr. Patel looked at Colonel Michaels and said, "You are so unperceptive."

Colonel Michaels turned angrily toward Julien and said, "This is completely irresponsible. You are endangering these women and these children. I expected more professionalism from you. Once was enough, now another baby with another colleague? Are you mad?"

"Why are you making me the bad guy?" responded Julien as he reached out to touch Andrea's arm.

Andrea was disgusted and threw her fork down into her plate, grabbed her baby, and stormed out of the dining area, yelling at Julien, "Don't touch me. Don't ever touch me again!"

"Andrea, baby, wait!" Julien called after her.

"Don't ever call me 'baby,' You have somewhere else to go now."

Julien followed her into her room but returned quickly, looking very anxious as Andrea threw him out and slammed the door behind him.

Colonel Michaels looked at him and said, "Words cannot convey how disappointed I am in you, Julien."

Julien replied, "Colonel, I am sorry…"

"It's too late for apologies," responded the colonel.

"This had to be preplanned," remarked Julien.

"What are you talking about?" asked the colonel angrily.

"This whole thing, Colonel Michaels. Don't you think this was some kind of planet repopulation scheme? We were sent here without the right pills. We were duped into having sex with each other. The powers that be knew that the planet maybe had no human life left, and they were counting on nature taking its course."

Dr. Patel responded to Julien's suggestion. "I doubt it. This was never part of their plan. They would have exercised more caution about crew selection if they wanted us to get pregnant. As you can see, Colonel Michaels and I are here too, and we are too old to be parents, even if we wanted to be."

Colonel Michaels looked at Denise reproachfully. "Denise, you should have known and acted better, too. You are as much at fault as Julien. This is irresponsible and also unfair to Andrea. You do not have the slightest clue of the peril you are putting this child in."

Chapter 16

Our Biology Is Our Destiny

TIME REMAINING				
YEARS	***DAYS***	***Hours***	***Minutes***	***Seconds***
13	***220***	***10***	***41***	***33***

Denise was in no mood for a lecture and her eyes shot daggers at the colonel as her voice grew louder.

"Look, Colonel, I don't need a sermon from you or anyone. I know why we came here. What do you expect us to do? Behave like machines and have no life for 16 years? I don't need a lesson in morality or ethics or whatever. I would expect some sympathy from you, at least. I did not mean for any of this to happen, it just happened. I am sorry if it upsets everyone. Everyone has a partner here, and I am by myself."

Colonel Michael tried calming her down. "Denise, please calm down. I was just…"

Denise cut him off and continued her rant. "I work in the woods all day and night, staring at trees. Then I come back here and stare at video footage for hours. I do not have a life at all. What else is there to do in the forest? Everyone has a partner here but me. You and your sweetheart, Dr. Patel, are a couple, even though you pretend not to be. I am spending the better part of my life in this God-forsaken wilderness doing nothing but watching grass grow. I am human, too. So, leave me alone!"

She was almost screaming now, and Andrea couldn't help but hear her as she sat in her own room wondering how to react.

Denise stormed off to her room but paused at her doorway and yelled back at the crew sitting in the kitchen, "God has damned all of us; he has forsaken us and left us here for dead like the rest of humanity!"

Colonel Michaels turned to Dr. Patel and suggested, "Maybe you should try to calm Denise and Andrea down, Arpita."

Dr. Patel replied, "I will have a word with them tomorrow. They both need their space now, and time to cry tonight."

The Colonel nodded and said, "I will be in my room if anyone needs me."

"I am signing off for the night too. I'll see you all in the morning," Dr. Patel muttered as she made her way back to her bedroom.

Just when everything had quieted down, and everyone was returning to their respective rooms, Denise emerged again and made another loud and startling pronouncement.

"Listen, everyone! I never wanted kids, and I don't want one now! I volunteered for this mission knowing that it meant never having kids. I want Dr. Patel to give me some abortion pill or perform an abortion herself. I'm not having this child. So, none of you need to worry about it."

Denise then turned and slammed her bedroom door shut. Dr. Patel and Colonel Michaels stood frozen in their bedroom doorways. They looked at each other, knowing this was guaranteed to bring on another clash.

Colonel Michaels looked over at Dr. Patel and said, "Do you want to discuss this?"

Dr. Patel replied, "No, I'm going to sleep on it, and I'll talk to Andrea and Denise tomorrow."

The Colonel wondered what Dr. Patel would do. Denise seemed adamant that she was not going to have this baby, and he knew Dr. Patel was just as determined never to perform an abortion. His lifelong interest in philosophy brought to mind the old paradox of the unstoppable spear meeting the impenetrable shield.

The next morning, Liz, Willie, Julien, Colonel Michaels and Dr. Patel all met at the breakfast table. By this time, Andrea and Denise were usually awake and enjoying breakfast, but both women were shut up in their rooms. Julien looked like he'd rather be anywhere else but there at that moment, and he turned to Willie and said, "I think I'll help you weed the gardens today."

Willie responded, "I just weeded it all yesterday. The gardens are pretty clean right now."

Julien shot back, "Well, I'll help you do something outside. I think I need to lie low for a while."

Dr. Patel got up and said, “I’m going to talk to them.” She walked over to Andrea’s room and gently knocked on the door. Andrea invited her in.

The doctor took a deep breath and stepped through the bedroom door. Andrea was sitting on the edge of her bed, holding Kristina. Before Dr. Patel said a word, Andrea began to speak. “I thought I had an exclusive relationship with Julien; maybe that was stupid. But I felt like I had been stabbed in the heart by the people closest to me.”

Dr. Patel spoke to Andrea in a calm and concerned voice. “Andrea, please listen to me. I understand that you are upset, but you know, Denise is our friend and part of our family, really. Do not take this to heart. She is very upset about this, too. You heard her screaming last night.”

Andrea leaned over and picked up a brush and began running it gently through her baby’s hair. “I just cannot get over the fact that she betrayed me. How could she do that? I feel so deceived by her.”

Dr. Patel responded in an almost dismissive tone, “You are a big girl, you know how the world works. You put a young man and a young woman in each other’s company morning, noon, and night, and something is going to happen. Nature guarantees it.”

“Yes” responded Andrea, “While that is all true, I believe moral decency demands that we rise above nature, don’t you think?”

“Sometimes things do not happen the way we expect,” asserted the doctor. “The greater part of maturity is learning how to react rationally when the unexpected happens. That being said, we are all going to be mothers and fathers to all these children, and by that, I mean Liam, Kristina, and Denise's child too. They are all 'our' children."

"I can't think about that right now," Andrea replied. "I am just not in that frame of mind."

"Andrea, come on now, please. You and Denise are best friends. Forgive her. You know these things can happen, especially when we are put in these situations. None of us ever anticipated anything like this would occur. Now, please come out to the kitchen. Kristina is hungry and I bet you are as well."

Dr. Patel then stepped out of Andrea's room and glanced over at the colonel sitting at the table in the kitchen. She shook her head and shrugged. Then she stepped over to Denise's door and knocked. Denise beckoned her in.

"How are you feeling?" Dr. Patel asked.

"Does everyone in the crew hate me?" Denise asked.

"Oh, come on now. Don't be ridiculous! We all love you, including Andrea, and I mean it. It was just a surprise for everyone. The first babies also took us by surprise. Colonel Michaels has become a father figure for all of us here, and this is why he worries so much about you and the rest of us. He carries everyone's problems on his back. If he sounded reproachful yesterday, he didn't mean it."

The doctor paused for a moment and then continued, "I'm sure this will have some negative impact on your relationship with Andrea for a while, but you both love each other, so this will pass. Julien is already hiding. I don't think he knows what to do. The three of you have to work this out. And I'm confident you will. After all, you have no choice. I am not a relationship counselor, and what's done is done. Honestly, it is very hard to have a private life here when we are all living so very close to each other."

The doctor allowed a few seconds for her words to sink in before proceeding in a reassuring tone. "The sun will come out tomorrow, and we will have babies to take care of. Isn't that exciting! I believe nothing could be more exciting. Otherwise, our lives would be routine and boring. It's good to have problems at times and believe me when I say this, a new baby is a good problem to have. Now, come with me and get something to eat. I will make you a nice omelet."

"I swear you surprise me, Dr. Patel. How come you always know the right thing to say at the right time! I am starving! But this problem is only temporary. I do not want to have this baby, so please give me some sort of pill to terminate this pregnancy. The other girls were happy to have a baby, but I never wanted one. There will be Liam and Kristina here when we leave, a boy and a girl, and they don't need any future complications by adding a third party to the mix."

"Don't be hasty," replied the doctor. "You are talking about a little baby. Think about it."

Denise had made up her mind to terminate the pregnancy. She could sense that Dr. Patel was unmovably against it. But it was her decision to make, and she had made it. She hoped Dr. Patel could be pressured into changing her mind.

She walked into the kitchen with Dr. Patel and a minute later, Andrea emerged, carrying Kristina. They both sat at the table as Dr. Patel made each of them breakfast. The morning passed without either Denise or Andrea saying a word to each other.

The days passed with every one of the crew keeping largely to themselves. There was still tension in the air. Later one evening, the tension gave way to yelling.

Everyone had settled down in front of the television to watch a movie. It was Colonel Michael's week to select the movie everyone would watch, and he picked an old Marx Brother's comedy. He felt that the crew needed something to lighten the mood. Julien and Andrea, who normally sat next to each other on the couch, were sitting apart. Denise and Dr. Patel were not there; they had retreated to the medical area to talk. The colonel decided to start the movie anyway, figuring the two of them needed to discuss things.

The movie had just begun when Denise's voice, growing ever louder, interrupted their viewing. "I don't care what you think!" Then a moment later, Denise's voice rang out again. "It is not your decision to make!"

At that point, no one was paying attention to the movie, and everyone was straining to hear what was going on in the next room between Dr. Patel and Denise. Although the doctor was speaking so quietly that no one could hear her end of the conversation, everyone could figure out the topic as they had no trouble hearing Denise.

"This is absurd! Maybe in India you could get away with it, but you can't get away with it here."

Suddenly, Denise emerged from the medical area and walked into the TV room. She looked flushed as she turned to the group and said, "Would you all mind leaving? I need to speak to Colonel Michaels privately."

Everyone jumped to their feet as if they couldn't clear out fast enough. They all returned to their rooms but left their bedroom doors open a crack, hoping to eavesdrop on the conversation between Denise and the colonel.

Denise stood over Colonel Michaels and said, "Dr. Patel is refusing to perform an abortion or give me any medication to terminate this pregnancy. You need to order her to do her job!"

The colonel sat motionless and didn't say a word.

Denise continued, "Did you hear me? You need to tell her to do her job!"

Everyone was listening by their doors. At one time or another during this mission, each of them had looked at Colonel Michaels and imagined that they could do as good a job leading the crew as he was doing. But at this moment, everyone was glad not to be in his position. He was the team leader, and he was facing a problem that seemed impossible to solve.

Colonel Michaels stood up and coaxed Denise to return with him to the medical area and talk to the doctor.

As Denise and the colonel entered the medical facility, they found Dr. Patel sitting at her desk with her hands clasped together, staring straight ahead. The colonel pulled up a chair and pointed, gesturing to Denise to have a seat. He then sat down between the two women.

"Denise wants you to give her an abortion, Arpita," Colonel Michaels began.

"I told you that I would never do that, and I told her the same thing," replied the doctor.

"Just order her to do it," blurted out Denise.

Dr. Patel didn't make eye contact with either of them but remained staring straight ahead. "I have already told Colonel Michaels that I would never perform an abortion, even if ordered to do so," Dr. Patel said firmly.

Denise shot back angrily, "You are the medical person here, you have to take care of all our medical situations. It is why you are here, goddamn it!"

Dr. Patel, trying to remain calm, repeated what she had already said to Denise. "You are not injured, and you are not sick. A pregnancy is not an illness to be cured."

"This is insane," Denise retorted as she slammed her hand on the desk. "I am not your slave; you cannot decide for me what I can and cannot do in this situation."

"Yes, that's right, responded the doctor. "And I am not your slave, and you cannot force me to do what you've decided you want in this situation. We have already had this conversation."

Colonel Michaels wanted to calm the women down as he searched for some sort of compromise. "Arpita, maybe there are some pills that will terminate the pregnancy. Just leave these pills out. Every member of the crew has access to the medical facility. They do not need your approval to take an aspirin. Denise can take these pills herself, and you'll have nothing to do with it. You'll bear no responsibility in this situation."

Dr. Patel responded, "There are no such medications here. With every ounce mattering, nothing we did not need was sent along. Pregnancies were never anticipated, so nothing like that was included in our supplies."

Denise now spoke in a quiet and calm voice. "Dr. Patel, I'm begging you please to do this for me."

The colonel looked at Dr. Patel, who turned and looked straight into Denise's eyes. "I'm sorry, I can't do what you ask."

Denise stood up and walked out of the medical area and straight to her room.

The next day was trying for everyone. At dinner, there was virtually no conversation. Colonel Michaels knew that Julien was squirming in his seat every time Denise or Andrea were in the room. He was at a loss on how to resolve the issue, and he hoped the two of them would somehow figure something out.

The following morning, the three men were in the garden and Julien asked, "Hey Colonel, you read those big fat philosophy books. What advice did they give you to resolve a situation like this?"

The colonel thought for a second and responded, "Remember that fat book I was reading, titled *Our Human Herds?* It suggested that in difficult circumstances, the needs of the individual are subordinated to the needs of the group. So, in poorer, more dangerous times, all men are expected to fight and defend the group, and all women expected to have babies to repopulate it. Personal preferences don't matter. It was as if our bodies belonged to the group first, and ourselves second. But, as society grew richer and safer, these social responsibilities waned, and things turned around: our bodies belonged to ourselves first, and society second. It is no coincidence that the military draft ended at about the time abortions were legalized. The bodies of both men and women were turned over to them individually, at the same time."

"That high-brow stuff sounds all well and good. But I don't think Denise is going to be convinced that she needs to have her baby for the good of the group," remarked Willie.

"I think you are right," answered the colonel. But one line from the book has always stuck in my mind, and maybe it's applicable here."

"Yeah? What's that?" asked Julien.

"Morality doesn't get us into heaven; morality keeps life on earth from becoming hell."

Julien nodded his head as he bent over to pull up a small weed.

That evening at dinner, and to do everyone a favor, the colonel came up with a plan that he had been up half the night putting together.

"The events of the past few days have forced us to suspend drone operations. But our primary mission remains to find people.

That requirement has not changed. Toward this end, I've developed a plan of further exploration. I want Willie and Julien to take one of the four-wheelers and proceed due east. The maps we were provided with tell us that about 80 miles east of here you should run into the Savannah River. I don't think a major waterway would have changed its course much in 9000 years. There is a more than even chance that if people do live around here, they will be making their homes near rivers or close to the ocean."

The colonel continued, "With that in mind, I want you two to follow the river southward about 50 additional miles, to the Atlantic Ocean. Then, proceed further south, following the coast, for about another 50 miles, and then head back northwest to our compound. When you get within 45 miles of the compound, a homing beacon will guide you back. On this circuitous mission, you will encompass about 4000 square miles of territory. I feel confident that you will eventually find some people or some remnant of their civilization."

Both Julien and Willie sat up in their chairs, excited by the chance to try something new and explore a distant area.

"You will bring along rifles, as you will have to hunt for most of your food." The colonel continued, "You will only be able to carry tents, knives, and a few basic supplies. The trip will be arduous, and I wouldn't expect you back for at least three to four weeks."

Willie had a question: "If we find people, what should we say to them. Do we approach them?"

"Absolutely not," said the colonel. "Two armed men emerging from the woods are likely to be seen as hostile. If you find a settlement, mark it precisely on your map. When you return, we'll send out a second party directly to that location with one of the women, probably Liz, who is our language expert. If we walk out of the woods with a woman, we are much less likely to appear hostile or threatening."

"Do you think they are going to be far advanced of us, or primitive?" wondered Willie.

"If they are advanced, they will certainly be able to take care of the children when we leave, and if they are primitive, we will learn valuable techniques on how to survive in this wilderness. Primitive or advanced, the children will benefit from their discovery."

Julien seemed overjoyed at the prospect of getting away for a while. He turned to Willie and said, "Come on, let's go make a list of supplies right now. We'll leave at first light."

That night, Liz was talking to Willie, urging him to be careful and return safely. Then she changed the subject and asked, "Don't you think Dr. Patel is wrong for not granting Denise's wish for an abortion?"

Willie responded in a sardonic tone, "Well, my animal husbandry background informs me that nature has already decided the issue. Every woman has two baby bottles hanging off the front of her body. They are not there for nothing."

Liz was taken aback by the crass remark. "And nature has also provided us with the superior intelligence that allows us to transcend our animal nature," she replied. "Two baby bottles I don't even know how to respond to that remark."

Willie, never wanting to go against anything Liz felt strongly about, backtracked immediately. "Of course, if Denise wants that, she should be able to get it. An abortion, I mean."

At the crack of dawn, Willie and Julien packed up their gear and headed off.

The following days found Denise extra quiet. One afternoon, Dr. Patel approached the colonel. "I know Denise has been looking through my medical computer files for drugs that might cause a spontaneous abortion. We have nothing specifically for that, but there are a few medications that may cause problems during pregnancy. I've hidden those away, as they are just as dangerous to the mother as to her unborn child."

The colonel just shook his head and said, "Given time, I hope she resigns herself to having this baby."

A week passed when one night, as Denise lay on her back staring straight up at the ceiling, she began recalling her life and how she ended up as a member of this crew. She remembered how her father and mother were divorced when she was young; how he had married another woman and had hardly ever called her. When she was little, she spent a few summers with his new family, but after a while, her only contact with her dad was a phone call on her birthday and Christmas presents that would arrive in the mail.

She thought of her mother, who never remarried. Denise was an only child, and her mother doted on her. Her mother was her constant companion and cheerleader, never failing to tell her that she was the prettiest, smartest, and most talented kid in all of her classes. She recalled going to college and enjoying taking the courses that were dominated by boys, like archeology and anthropology. She thought about her past boyfriends. But her relationships had always been brief and casual.

Not having had any long-term relationships, the thought of family life and motherhood had never really occupied her mind. Nor did it interest her. She loved her studies and her schoolwork. She became a professor for a while, teaching at a university, and later was recruited by NASA. All the time her mother stood by, visiting when she could, regardless of where she moved to.

She recalled the night before she left on this mission, talking to her mother on the phone, and how her mother was crying when saying goodbye. But she had been so excited about the adventure, she didn't seem to give her mother's emotional reaction much notice. The last words she said to her were, "I love you mom, and I'll see you in 16 years!"

Now she wondered how her mother was doing. Her mother was 57 when she left, and there was no guarantee she'd be alive when Denise returned. As these thoughts were coursing through her head, she felt a tear slide down each side of her face. She didn't realize she was tearing up and how much she loved and missed her mother until that moment. She resolved that if she was going to have this baby, she was going to love it and cheer for it as her mother had always done for her. She also resolved to name it after her mother: Stephanie.

Somehow, thinking of her mother, and thinking of naming her baby after her, made coming to terms with having the child a little easier.

A couple of days passed.

The atmosphere seemed lighter with Julien and Willie absent. One evening, after everyone had gone to bed, Denise heard a gentle knock on her door.

"Yes, who is it?" Denise inquired.

Andrea replied, "It's me. Can I come in?"

"Yes, come on in."

Both women looked at each other for a few seconds with silent stares.

Andrea then sat down next to Denise on her bed and began, "I just wanted to tell you that I don't think God has forsaken this place -- or us. And that I am happy for you and your baby. We are such a small group. It's like every baby belongs to all of us anyway."

"I appreciate that," replied Denise. Andrea and Denise embraced each other warmly.

Denise, pulled back and smiled, "My goal is to be as good a mother as you are."

"Denise, I am very sure you will be wonderful!" said Andrea.

“And I think I know why all women eventually say they hate men,” Denise laughed.

“We can agree on that,” smiled Andrea.

Chapter 17

Another Tragedy

TIME REMAINING				
YEARS	***DAYS***	***Hours***	***Minutes***	***Seconds***
13	***185***	***11***	***41***	***30***

With the absence of Julien and Willie, the compound took on a much quieter aspect.

Sitting down at the table for breakfast, Liz exclaimed to the others, "I never realized how much commotion those two caused."

She continued, "For dinner tonight, I think I'll make the last of the fish Willie and Julien had caught and frozen before they left. I bet when they get back, they'll be starving and craving a homecooked meal."

As she jumped up and disappeared into the other room, Andrea remarked, "They've been gone for weeks! I wonder where they are now."

She returned a minute later with her laptop computer. "This computer is tied into the main computing station in the compound. If the guys are within 45 miles, the computer will pick up the homing beacon built into their four-wheeler and will guide them back."

"Those vehicles are amazing," interjected the colonel. "They can travel hundreds of miles on a charge, and have built-in solar panels to keep them operating almost indefinitely."

"Oh, here they are," Andrea said with excitement as she pointed to a red blip on her computer screen. "They are only about 12 miles away. Even at the slow rate those four-wheelers move through our woods, I still expect them to be home tonight or tomorrow. I wonder what they found?"

"Can't you send out a drone to find them?" asked Denise.

"That's a wonderful idea," replied Andrea. "I'll do it as soon as I'm done eating."

When the group finished with breakfast, Andrea launched one of her drones in the direction of the homing signal emitted continuously by the four-wheeler. She found Julien and Willie within an hour. Hovering 25 feet over their heads, the drone sent back pictures of the boys bouncing along, riding atop a rocky precipice about 15 feet above a stream. The boys spotted the drone right away and waived enthusiastically up at it.

The crew were all gathered around the computer screen looking at the men. "They seem glad and even excited to be heading back," noted Andrea. "I can't wait to hear about what they've seen."

The girls and Colonel Michaels resumed their daily routines with everyone anxious to hear the stories Willie and Julien would return with, and probably exaggerate. Colonel

Michaels had been doing his best to keep Willie's gardens free of weeds, but he was sure Willie would be disappointed upon his return. "No one can take care of these plants and animals like Willie does," he thought to himself.

Suddenly he heard a voice from behind him. "How are you doing?" It was Dr. Patel coming to check on the colonel and see what he was up to.

"Willie planted these gardens just before he left, and I'm afraid I've already allowed them to be overrun with weeds," the colonel lamented. "I'm afraid I'm not much of a farmer."

Later that afternoon, Andrea noticed that the red blip on her computer screen had hardly moved from the spot where it had been that morning. Concerned, she immediately sent her drone back out to find the guys. It was almost dark when she came upon a sight that made her blood run cold.

"Colonel, Dr. Patel, come here quickly," she yelled.

Everyone heard her worried cry and rushed to her side. They found Andrea staring into the computer screen, looking at the horrible image sent back by her drone. They all stood speechless.

The drone hovered above the four-wheeler, submerged upside down in the stream. All that could be seen sticking out of the water was the top of the rear wheels and the rear bumper where the homing beacon was located and still sending out its signal.

Trembling with fear, Andrea said, "This looks like the spot where we saw them this morning. This must have happened only minutes after we brought the drone back. They must have accidentally driven off the ledge above the stream and tumbled into the water. Oh my God, I hope they're alright."

She felt a wave of guilt wash over her. "What if waiving at my drone caused them to look away from where they were going? What if I caused them to have this accident?"

She immediately began directing her drone to search the area near the site where the four-wheeler was overturned in the stream. But it was getting dark and little could be seen.

The colonel said, "At first light, I'll take one of the other vehicles out to their location." He didn't want to alarm the others, but thought to himself, "If those two were wearing their seat belts when the vehicle tumbled into the stream, they would've been trapped under it and submerged. They might both be dead."

Though it had become too dark to see anything from the drone's camera, everyone remained gathered around the computer looking at the darkened screen.

Not wanting to alarm the others, Colonel Michaels casually wandered into the other room and motioned to Dr. Patel to join him. He turned to her with a worried look and whispered, "If they tumbled into that creek strapped into their seats, they would have been trapped under that vehicle, under the water. We may never be able to get their bodies out."

He paused for a moment and then went on, "If they are dead, our continued existence here will be in jeopardy. Those two guys did most of the hard work, keeping up with the gardens and taking care of the animals, hunting, and everything else. Without them, I don't know how we're going to make it."

"Don't give up hope," Dr. Patel implored in a hush.

Andrea turned and yelled to Colonel Michaels. "I'm recalling that drone and sending out another. I set it to send us back infrared images. If they are anywhere in the area, we may find them through their body heat."

An hour later, the infrared-seeking drone was in the area of the stream searching for Julien and Willie. No one considered sleeping and the search went on into the night. Finally, around midnight, one of them was spotted.

"Here is one of them, lying on the ground. It is a clear outline of a man," exclaimed Andrea.

"Can you see which one it is?" asked Liz.

"No." Andrea responded. "But I can tell that there is only one person there."

Everyone gathered around the infrared image, and each sadly confirmed that there was only one person revealed on the screen. Everyone knew that if both had survived, they'd be together.

"He is about a mile from the crash site. He must be alright if he walked that far. I'm sure I will be able to guide you to him in the morning," Andrea said, her voice trembling a bit.

As soon as the first rays of light appeared on the horizon, Colonel Michaels and Dr. Patel headed out toward the location of the crash. Andrea's drone had been switched over to visual light and through the canopy she could see Willie looking up waiving at the drone.

Liz was amazed and relieved, it appeared that Willie was safe. She felt as if her prayers had been answered. But what of the prayers of Denise and Andrea? Liz was almost afraid to look into the faces of the other women.

It took most of the morning to get there, but finally the colonel spotted Willie.

To his happy amazement, sitting next to him on the ground was Julien.

"Oh, my Lord, are we ever happy to see both of you alive!" shouted Dr. Patel.

"The four-wheeler slid off the embankment and tumbled into the stream," explained Willie. "Neither of us were wearing our seat belts, thank God, and we were both thrown from the vehicle, but the roll bar crashed down on Julein's foot. We think it's broken."

Willie and the colonel each took one of Julien's arms over their shoulder and carefully hobbled him into the vehicle. He was in so much pain he could hardly speak.

"When we get back, I'll attend to your foot right away," the doctor assured him.

"His foot had swollen so much, I had to cut it out of his boot," Willie explained. "We wrapped it in some fabric. It's not bleeding but it's incredibly swollen."

"We found you with the infrared camera last night," the colonel told them. "But the camera only saw one of you. We thought the worst, and that maybe only one of you had survived."

"Willie covered me with a plastic tarp he managed to salvage from our four-wheeler," replied Julien. It was damp last night, and cold. I covered myself with it; everything but by nose. Willie lay beside me shivering. I guess that's why you only saw one of us. You could see the heat from Willie's body, but not mine."

"Do you have any water?" Julien asked.

"Both of you guys are probably dehydrated. Here's a canteen of water; drink as much as you can," instructed the doctor.

Back at the compound, and through the drone's camera, the women saw both Willie and Julien being loaded into the vehicle. Their hearts lept in joy. They hugged each other and could hardly control their excitement.

"I'm going to kiss both of them when they get back," grinned Andrea.

"And I'm going to promise not to tell them how lazy and worthless they are – at least for a week," laughed Liz.

Denise joined in. "I bet they'll be starving when they get home. Let's make them a nice dinner."

At dusk, the colonel, Dr. Patel, and the boys finally got back. Julien was in so much pain he could hardly move. Denise, Andrea, and Liz hadn't realized that Julien had been hurt. They all pounded him with questions about what happened. Dr. Patel waived at them to be quiet and directed them to help get Julien to the medical area. There they unwrapped his foot and winced as they noticed some of the toes on his right foot had been crushed.

Sending the others away, the doctor pointed to Liz, "This is a very serious contusion. Let's you and I take care of Julien. Set up an intravenous drip from the medical supplies."

Within a few minutes, Doctor Patel was hydrating Julien. She added an anesthetic to the intravenous fluid and instructed Liz to monitor his heart rate and breathing closely.

"This is a new 'universal' anesthetic and potent anodyne," the doctor said to Liz. "But in cases like this, I wish I had some of the old-style morphine. However, this stuff is supposed to be the best. It's a pain killer in tiny doses, and an anesthetic in larger ones. Now let's get a look at this foot."

The two women maneuvered the portable x-ray machine over and noted that the two smaller digits on Julien's right foot had been crushed. Both were blackened badly from a buildup of blood and bone splinters. "I'm going to have to take these two toes off," said the doctor.

"What do you mean?" asked Liz.

"I mean amputation. Keep him sedated."

Liz and the doctor sterilized their hands and Julien's foot and leg, and with the help of computer tutorials, quickly removed the two smaller toes from Julien's right foot. They sutured and bandaged it and stayed with him as he slept for hours.

The next morning, everyone awoke still tired and dragging from the trauma the day before. All wanted to know the details about Julien. Dr. Patel told them of the ghastly injury to Julien's foot and what needed to be done.

Andrea went in and sat by Julien's side until he awoke two hours after everyone else. She told him what happened and what needed to be done. The medical facility was equipped with a pair of crutches, and in a short while Julien was up, limping and shuffling around.

The colonel and the girls were anxious to know the details of their adventure and if any trace of other people had been found. The men assured them that they had been diligent in their search, but found not a single trace of humanity.

As a sort of devilish compensation, they made everyone's mouths water as they spoke in rich detail of finding clams, shrimp, crabs, and other seafood delights that they had not enjoyed for years.

"I had almost forgotten how good shrimp tasted," nodded Julien. "They were almost worth losing a few toes over."

With his ubiquitous sense of humor returning, Julien's relaxed attitude in the face of his severe suffering made everyone feel more at ease.

Scratching and itching as they recounted their journey, it was apparent that the men had contracted a rather bad case of lice from being away so long and having to sleep outdoors. Luckily, insecticides had been provided and they were quickly deloused. Before long, their incessant scratching eased.

During the following week, Dr. Patel provided Julien with painkillers and antibiotics. He was soon back to his old self.

Always the clown, he would come up alongside Andrea, Liz, or Denise and put an arm around their shoulder laying his heavy weight on them, saying that since losing his two toes, his weight was no longer evenly distributed on his body and that he needed them to help hold him up.

And every time someone mentioned the operation, Julien moaned as if in emotional distress crying out, "Woe is me," and while pretending to cry would say things like: "I keep trying to forget about my horrible disfigurement but you terrible people remind me of it!"

With the two guys back and as lighthearted as ever, the compound returned to its noisy-but-normal routine. Willie told Julien he was giving him the week off from helping with the gardens and with the animals, but warned he'd not let him milk his injury for any longer than that.

The safe return of the boys made the crew's other problems pale to insignificance.

Denise eventually gave birth to her baby. It turned out to be a boy. She named him Stephen, after her mother.

As before, the men instinctively turned and looked at the chronometer to see how old this baby would be when the crew departed.

TIME REMAINING				
YEARS	***DAYS***	***Hours***	***Minutes***	***Seconds***
13	***1***	***10***	***41***	***33***

Liz, Andrea, and Denise were all mothers now. And Dr. Patel was happily involved every day in caring for, and loving, each of the children. She seemed like a second mother to all of them.

The men would all go on to share an avuncular relationship with the kids. The children were a source of constant amusement to everyone..

Exploration continued in all directions, but more and more, it was family life and child rearing that defined their lives.

Chapter 18

Say It Ain't So

TIME REMAINING				
YEARS	***DAYS***	***Hours***	***Minutes***	***Seconds***
7	*343*	*17*	*20*	*44*

The crew had now spent close to eight years searching for any remnant of humanity. Over half their stay was behind them with no traces of what might have happened being discovered. They had traveled north to where they imagined Atlanta had been, and found nothing. There was talk of making an enormous trek to the known locations of Washington D.C., or even New York City. But the venture was impractical, given the equipment they had been provided.

Life had become routine. The children were getting older, and the future was everybody's home now. Few ever thought of the past, and returning to it seldom crossed their minds. Liam was already seven years old, Kristina followed close behind, and Stephen was almost five. The adults were excited to learn and then teach the children the skills needed to survive without 21st century aid.

When the children were little, the adults would often talk about learning the skills needed to survive in the wild. But up until recently they had made only a half-hearted attempt to acquire them. But now that the kids were getting older, the adults took the task more seriously. They grew determined to learn how to survive in the wilderness and to pass on the skills to their offspring.

Willie showed the kids how to plant the garden with plows made from modified sticks fashioned out of the hardest wood he could find. The two older children were getting to the age where they could understand what they were being taught. He refused to use the metal hoe or farm equipment provided with the compound.

Willie was more diligent than the others about using only the implements that would be available to the children after the crew was gone.

Learning how to plant and reap seemed like a game to them. They enjoyed learning every new thing, though their little hands tired quickly. No one worked harder than Willie, and he relished the praise he received from the rest of the crew for his determination.

He taught them that they needed to save at least 10 percent of the seeds they harvested from every crop for use in planting the next year's corn, wheat, and potatoes. He showed them how to prevent the food from being eaten by field mice or other animals. Because the children were still young, each lesson had to be repeated often. But the adults didn't seem to mind any amount of repetition where the children were concerned.

Julien spent his time searching for, and experimenting with, just the right rocks that would take easily to sharpening.

He had almost perfected the ideal spear point and arrowhead. But from working with sharp objects all day, the men routinely returned to the compound with cuts, some severe, acquired when a shard of flint or obsidian sliced through a palm, or when a sharpened stick penetrated a foot. They were careful to teach the children safety precautions to avoid such injuries when no doctor would be there to treat them.

Today Willie and Julien were having a good time with the makeshift kiln they put together from mud bricks, doing their best to master the art of pottery making.

"Damn! I thought I had it!" shouted Julien, as he reached into the hot oven and tried to pull out a piece of pottery. The guys continued to wrestle the clay pot from the makeshift kiln using two sticks. As they brought it to the edge, it fell to the ground and shattered.

Both Willie and Julien shouted, "Damn!"

Denise, bending over some kindling and rubbing sticks together, was attempting to start a fire. Unable to make any progress, she threw down the sticks and picked up two rocks made from flint and banged them together. Frustrated, she threw the rocks down too.

"Jesus Christ! How can I make a fire by banging two rocks together? How can something so simple become so complicated?" She trudged back into the compound to take a break and regain her composure.

A while later, Willie and Julien pulled out another pot from the fire and watched it crumble. They looked at each other in disgust. “Let’s go get some lunch,” suggested Julien, “and we’ll come back out later and try again.”

The days passed by quickly. Each crew member kept busy trying to master some skill they knew the children would need after they were gone. Love became the great motivator, and every time anyone became discouraged, they would look at the children and start again.

Julien eventually grew quite adept at finding just the right stones to create arrowheads and spear points without shedding a drop of his own blood. Unlike the adults, the children seemed to master every task in short order.

As winter approached, Willie recognized that shelter was going to be one of the most important requirements for survival. With the cold setting in, and little to do in the garden, he set his mind on figuring out how to make a hut from reeds, mud, and grass. He meticulously gathered just the perfect material and had already become familiar with the consistency of certain clays from his experience making pottery with Julien.

He began assembling his material outside, about ten yards from the compound’s front door. For a number of days, whenever anyone stepped outside, they’d find Willie putting together his hut. “How’s it going today?” they’d each inquire. “It’s going to be the Taj Mahal of mud huts,” he’d yell back and laugh.

Finally, it was completed and looked perfect. The next morning, Willie and the colonel were the first ones up. The crew had become accustomed to drinking hot tea at breakfast, as the coffee supply they were provided had run out long ago. “I do miss a good cup of coffee,” the colonel muttered.

"Hey, I think it's starting to rain," said Willie.

"This will be a good time to test out your masterpiece," smiled the colonel.

Both men walked over to the front door and opened it. They stood in the doorway to see what effect the rain would have on Willie's hut.

Willie looked at Colonel Michaels and said, "Oh man. That's the best-looking hut made in these here woods in a thousand years, I bet."

The Colonel agreed, "It does look great, Willie. An excellent job, I congratulate you!"

"It took me two days to gather the materials and three full days to finish the hut. I am confident it will work well."

"It looks like it's starting to rain harder," remarked the colonel. "This will be a real test."

Standing in the doorway, both men looked on as Willie's pride-and-joy slowly collapsed and fell apart, sinking slowly into a giant puddle of mud. Willie, sounding a little dejected, turned to Colonel Michaels and asked rhetorically, "If we are all so smart and well-trained, how come we can't even figure out how to live like cavemen?"

TIME REMAINING				
YEARS	***DAYS***	***Hours***	***Minutes***	***Seconds***
7	***250***	***1***	***22***	***24***

Everyone was sitting around the dinner table and Denise was the first to speak. “I have come to a very stark and exciting realization. I believe we do not have to raise our children with all the prejudices and hang-ups of the 21st century. We can pretty much start the world over, you could say.”

Andrea asked, “I don’t understand what you mean by prejudices and hangups.”

“What I mean is,” continued Denise “looking at our children playing outside, I could already see the boys being comfortable not wearing shirts on hot days while your little girl is wearing one. They are mimicking our way of life where the men casually walk around without wearing shirts, but we ladies must not.”

Andrea, looking a little puzzled, inquired, “I am not sure what you mean. What are you suggesting?”

Denise then smiled and said, “You know. Well, I mean, all of us should be completely okay being topless. By that, I mean all of us, men and women alike. If the boys can be topless, why not the girls? Kristina is too young to know the difference and the boys are still small. Let us all be comfortable being topless and it will become natural to them.”

Liz smiled widely, "I am perfectly fine with the idea. I will go topless!"

Willie looked at Liz and said, "Hell no you won't!"

Andrea then interrupted. "I am sorry, I will not do that."

Dr. Patel looked stunned and added, "I'm not doing that either."

Julien smiled too and said, "I'm game. I am in complete favor of equality in all its shapes and sizes."

The subject was dropped, and Andrea continued to make sure little Kristina wore a top whenever she went outside or was around the boys. Colonel Michaels reminded the group that our "traditions" become our "morals" if they are practiced long enough.

The mission was well past its halfway point, and everyone could be found occasionally reflecting on how different it had turned out from what any of them could have anticipated.

The men eventually perfected the skill of making bow strings and fish traps. The women continued hard at work identifying all the edible plants in the area and devising recipes, making sure only to use wild-grown ingredients. After being heard to express every profanity she had ever known, Denise finally mastered the art of making a fire, and she could whip one up pretty quickly when needed. She learned that fires made from hardwoods like maple and oak burned hotter than fires made from pines.

Boiling water for soups was a particularly arduous task that took months to master. A bladder of water was placed near a fire while rocks were heated. When the rocks were red-hot, they were removed from the fire with a forked stick and dropped into the water. Sometime the rocks would explode, which was quite dangerous. She hated having the children attempt this, but necessity overruled worry.

Denise had begun as the group's seamstress, but Andrea quickly learned that she too was quite adept at designing garments and sewing them together – "garments," of course, being animal skin loin clothes and fur moccasins. The women tried for years to learn how to weave the wool from the sheep into something they could use to make clothing but were never successful. The wool covered skins were the closest they could get. And they all tried to find some use for the chicken's feathers. But aside from insulation for the huts, or ornamentation on clothes, the feathers were not very good for anything.

The first day Colonel Michaels appeared before the group wearing only a beaver pelt loin cloth, he got a hearty laugh from everybody.

"Oh, if the guys at the officer's club could only see me now," he joked.

Julien roared with laughter. "I swear, Colonel, you look remarkably like Fred Flintstone!"

Like everyone else, Dr. Patel took care to involve the children in her activities. She took the lead in learning, and then teaching others, how to skin animals, separating their meat and organs from the bones and skin, and how to preserve them by drying or smoking.

Though electric stoves and microwave ovens had been provided with the compound, the women made sure that a fire was built using only sticks and stones and that at least one meal was prepared that way every day.

This was especially hard on cold or rainy days, but the women took it as a challenge to find dry kindling and get a fire started outdoors under any conditions and in all seasons. They taught the children to store dry wood and reeds on the dry days, so that they would have something to start a fire with on the wet ones.

Denise worked closely with Andrea, using her drones to find and identify medicinal herbs and plants in the area. The children were taken for walks through the woods and taught how to identify and use natural medicines to treat ailments. They were taught to use landmarks to find their way back to the compound, as well as which plants to avoid for fear of their thorns or toxins.

Andrea and Denise discovered that they had a penchant for weaving and creating baskets out of reeds and dried grasses. Soon, the girls had mastered using larger reeds and mud to create small huts and were doing a far better job than Willie. They dragged Liz into the venture, though she was always the most fastidious, forever complaining about getting mud in her hair and dirt under her fingernails.

Smearing mud on the walls of the huts became like a game and the children enjoyed playing it. With practice, the structures became quite cozy and weatherproof. It wasn't long before the children alone could start from nothing and build themselves a decent shelter with a warm fire in half a day.

All the adults marveled at just how much children could master at an early age. They often thought back on the world they came from, where children were hardly allowed to go outside and play without supervision, and how so little was expected of them before their teenage years. Yet these kids, not yet ten years old, were already building fires and making shelters.

The division of labor that had begun years ago was now in full force. The men spent their time learning to track animals and hunt. They preferred hunting larger game as it provided the most food for the growing members of the expanded family. It took a lot of strength to pull back hard enough on a homemade bow-and-arrow or throw a spear with enough force to pierce the body of a running deer or wild hog. And it took a fantastic amount of stamina to follow its blood trail for hundreds of yards through thorny underbrush until it finally died; and then, even more strength to throw a 95-pound deer's body over one's shoulders and carry it back to the compound.

Both the men and the women began to understand what primitive life was really like. It revolved mostly around the everyday necessities of finding food and keeping warm. Making spears, making bow strings from animal gut, and battling the elements to find food were everyday necessities. The females were even busier than the men, watching over the kids, keeping a fire constantly burning in all weather conditions, and taking the better part of a full day to prepare and cook a meal.

"I used to think our ancestors were just a lot of sexist pigs," said Denise as she dropped a hot stone into a bladder of water. "But I realize that they probably knew what they were doing."

"I guess they were not all domineering jerks after all," laughed Andrea.

The adults began rotating the task of sleeping once every few days outdoors in the huts with the children. At first, the kids liked the adventure, but, like everyone else, they soon complained and cried that they wanted to sleep inside. One of the big problems with sleeping outdoors was the ever-present abundance of mosquitoes, fleas, and ticks. Dr. Patel did a lot of research to identify plants with strong odors that, when smeared all over the body, helped keep insects away. Needless to say, the women were not thrilled at stinking it up but, like all mothers, they did what they had to do for the good of the children.

One evening, while everyone was gathered inside for dinner, Colonel Michaels exclaimed, "Oh my God, what is that horrible odor?"

"It's me," cried out Andrea, not knowing whether to laugh or cry. "Dr. Patel recognized that vinegar, which is pretty easy to make, is also great for keeping away insects. So, I've smeared it all over my body as a test, and I haven't had time to take a shower yet."

"I think it's going to keep away the rest of us too," teased the colonel.

Willie chimed in, "Yes, ferment any fruits or sugars and you first get wine, and after a while it turns to vinegar. Give me your empty perfume bottles and I'll fill them up for you."

Changing the subject, the colonel went on, "I've taken it upon myself to teach each of the children how to read and write. Though there will be no books to read once we have departed, I still feel that it is an important skill. I've used the bark of certain trees as paper, and I have them practice writing and doing arithmetic. Every night, after dinner and before a movie, I'm going to read something to them, or have them read on their own, or out loud to me."

Chapter 19

Fun Meets Danger

TIME REMAINING				
YEARS	***DAYS***	***Hours***	***Minutes***	***Seconds***
6	***333***	***8***	***27***	***53***

At first, the three children were always at the side of their parents. But as they grew older, they wandered farther away, running through the woods and playing games by themselves. The moms were always yelling at them to stay close by, but invariably, they strayed off to the edge of the woods or up the side of a nearby hill.

Their favorite place to play was up on the side of the large hill that overlooked the compound. On it was an enormous flat boulder that faced the facility – the surface was smooth enough to allow them to slide down and jump off at the end of it. An activity they never seemed to tire of.

Every day, they begged their moms to let them go play on the 'sliding stone.' But the mothers were not entirely at ease.

On one such occasion, Liz commented, "Even though we can look out the front door and see the kids playing in the distance on that stupid rock, I do not feel comfortable at all with them being so far away from us."

Andrea thought for a minute and piped up, “Eureka! I have a fantastic idea! I can program my drones to fly above their heads, and we can just watch them on the computer screen in the kitchen. I would just need to move my computer from the lab to the countertop here. They can go wherever they want, and we can monitor them on the screen.”

Denise thought for a moment and inquired, “That’s all nice and dandy, but what if they leave the sliding stone and wander elsewhere?”

Andrea beamed. “These drones are simply amazing. They can be programmed to follow the children wherever they venture off to. If they split up, the drones can then send us a signal. Plus, we can always get a tracking signal from the drone and find the kids should they get lost.”

“Will we be able to hear the kids at all?” Liz asked. “I mean, what if they get hurt or start to cry or something?”

“No, not really,” Andrea replied, hesitantly. “Well, maybe, but it would be too far off the ground to hear any words. The drone will have to come close to pick up any audio sources, but we can definitely create some sort of sign. We’ll tell the kids to wave their hands in the air and scream if they require any assistance or if they’re hurt or in trouble. It will be like a signal.”

Denise chuckled, “Those children are always waving their hands in the air, so that will be very confusing. We would assume they are in trouble every minute. Let’s think up a different gesture.”

“What if we teach them to clench both hands together and wave them up toward the drone?” Liz suggested. “This will be clear enough, and it’s not something they normally would do.”

Andrea’s face lit up. “That’s fantastic! Let’s teach the kids the signal, and I’ll reprogram a drone to hover about 70 feet above them at all times. And as long as one of us is in the kitchen, we’ll be able to watch them every minute. Furthermore, we’ll tell them to yell the word “OMMMM.” That’s what Kristina calls them. She can’t pronounce ‘drone,’ so she says, ‘OMM.’ Now all the kids call them ‘OMMS.’”

Denise had another thought. “What about the guys? When will it be their turn to watch the children?”

Liz laughed and said, “I think we would need to send up a second ‘OMM’ to watch the guys!”

Andrea’s drone system proved ingenious. It allowed the kids to be free to roam about while giving their mothers the peace of mind that came from being able to watch them every minute.

One hot afternoon, Liz and Willie were in the kitchen, and Willie noticed something on the monitor.

“Hey, isn’t that the help signal you taught the kids to use whenever they were in trouble?”

Liz looked at the monitor. The kids had their fists clenched together and were pumping them skyward toward the drone, yelling, “Omm! Omm! Omm!”

"Yes! Oh my God, Willie, something is wrong," she screamed.

"Relax. I know exactly where they are. It's the creek," said Willie as he rushed out the door.

Willie, with Liz close behind, raced out of the compound and rushed to the kids playing by the nearby stream.

They noticed that Liam was calling for help. "Mom! Dad! Help! Stevie has fallen into the creek, and we got him out, but he's not moving at all." Liam started to cry, "I think he's dead." Kristina pleaded with Willie and Liz, "Please help him."

Liz was a trained medical professional and immediately began giving him mouth-to-mouth resuscitation. Within only a few seconds Stephen began to cough and regained consciousness. It seemed that he had swallowed a lot of water but was otherwise completely fine. The children were amazed at how Liz had brought their little friend back to life.

Liz asked, "Stevie, honey, are you okay?"

Stephen coughed a bit and said, "Yes."

The adults took the children by the hand and began walking slowly back to the compound. Liz scolded them the entire way back. "We've told you not to go near this stream unless an adult was with you."

Stevie looked up and begged, "Please don't tell my mother that I fell into the creek. She'll kill me!"

"I'm going to tell your mother," Liz responded.

After the creek incident, the parents decided to give all the children swimming lessons. Before long, they were all paddling around like dolphins and seemed as comfortable in the water as out of it.

But the children were not the only ones involved in a bit of mischief. Two weeks after the drowning scare, Willie approached Julien near the rabbit pens. He had a wild look in his eyes.

> "Come back here with me Julien; I have something interesting to show you."

Julien followed Willie down a path seldom used toward the side of the compound. About 100 yards into the woods, they came across a clearing where Willie kept the makeshift still he used to create the apple cider vinegar they needed as insect repellant. He turned to Julien, handed him a small cup, and said, "Taste this."

Julien put the cup to his lips and took a sip. "Oh, this is awful!"

"I know! Isn't it great?" laughed Willie. "It's apple cider wine, the first step in making apple cider vinegar. A few cups of this and we'll forget all our troubles."

Julien took another sip and said, "Yuk! Is this the best you can do?"

The men had not tasted a single drop of alcohol in years. It didn't take long before they were both staggering, rolling on the ground, slurring their words, and laughing hysterically.

The children, who knew every bush, trail, and path for miles around, soon stumbled upon their fathers. They snuck up on the two men and peered through the bushes. They didn't know what to make of it; they had never seen their dads act like this. Liam turned to the other two and put his finger to his lips. "Shhh, let's go back and get our moms."

The kids ran back and found Andrea, Liz, and Denise crouching over a fire.

"Mom, come and see this, there is something wrong with dad and Julien," Liam yelled.

The women jumped to their feet and followed the kids down the path. When they peered through the brush and saw Willie and Julien laying on their back laughing, cups in their hands, next to the still, they quickly figured out what was going on.

Denise turned to Liz and Andrea and said, "Go get the colonel, and take these kids back with you."

A minute later the colonel showed up and peered through the bushes. Denise turned to the colonel and said, "If this happened right after we got here, I might have joined them. Now they just look like two jackasses."

The colonel turned to her and came up with one of his aphorisms that he had become known for,

"The years teach us much that the days never knew."

“Go back to the compound and tell Arpita to get an emetic ready,” he directed. “These two are probably going to need it.”

A moment later Julien and Willie looked up to find Colonel Michaels towering over them with his hands on his hips. “You boys are acting like fools. Your kids saw you and they think you’ve gone crazy.”

Willie lifted up his cup to the colonel and said, “Taste this, boss.”

The colonel took a sip and said, “Oh, this is horrible!”

“Ya, I know! Isn’t it great?” repeated Willie.

The colonel poured out what remained in the cup and said,

“You two come back to the compound and I trust this will never happen again.”

Before long, the two drunks stumbled back home. That night found them puking their guts out and moaning. The kids couldn’t help but overhear what was going on and they asked their moms about it. The moms invented some story about their dads trying a new berry that had not been confirmed as edible. They used the incident as an object lesson for the children, to be very careful about eating anything they were not familiar with. The men woke up the next morning with pounding headaches. The experience was so negative that they were never again tempted to whip up a batch of “Willie’s firewater” and get drunk.

Chapter 20

Time for a Reckoning

TIME REMAINING				
YEARS	*DAYS*	*Hours*	*Minutes*	*Seconds*
6	*298*	*1*	*22*	*24*

As had become the custom, the team gathered together nightly to watch a movie after dinner and after the kids had read with the colonel or Julien. Julien had found a copy of the Koran on his computer and wanted to read it to the children. Dr. Patel asked Colonel Michaels to include the Bhagavad Gita as part of his reading program with the kids too. Everyone wanted to be sure that the children would be prepared for life on their own physically, mentally, and spiritually.

The team had experienced so many highs and lows together that they were closer than the tightest family. Every day they spent hours together, laughing, crying, arguing, and apologizing. The love between the group was more than any of them had ever known before. Every funny incident brought them closer to each other.

One night, no different from any other, the group was gathering in front of the TV.

"I tell you what," announced Julien. "By the time we get back, Hollywood will be no more. As we were leaving, they were advertising the premiere of a movie created completely by artificial intelligence, where none of the characters in the film was actually a living person. They said you couldn't tell the difference. When we do get back, there will be no more movie stars! Won't that be weird?"

Everyone nodded.

Liz plopped down on the couch and asked, "Who is picking the movie tonight?"

Willie chimed in, "It was Colonel Michaels' turn to pick, but he said he had run out of choices, and I heard him ask Dr. Patel to pick it for him."

Denise sat up in her seat. "Oh no! I swear she picks the worst movies! The last time it was her turn she picked that Italian film with English subtitles, called *La Strada*. And, before that she picked some crazy flick from India called, *The Apu Trilogy*. I may just hit the sack early tonight."

Julien turned and asked her, "What didn't you like about *La Strada*? The movie was about this big, strong guy who beats and bullies a mentally impaired young girl and forces her into having sex with him while performing for crowds to earn him money. Then, he left her by the side of the road to die. What's not to like about that?"

Denise rolled her eyes and said, "You're either depraved or a nutcase."

Andrea laughed, "Here comes the dynamic duo, now."

Colonel Michaels and Dr. Patel walked into the room.

Dr. Patel looked around and said proudly, "I have a very famous and interesting movie picked out for us tonight. It is called *The Seventh Seal.* It's an old Swedish movie about a medieval knight who plays chess with the personification of death."

Denise leaned over and whispered to Andrea, "Please kill me now."

The following week, Liz and Willie began acting a little bizarre. Both were exceptionally quiet and seemed reluctant to interact with the rest of the crew. It was clear that something serious was being kept between them from the others.

The safe room had been converted into the children's bedroom and it was usually a mess. Days later, as the mothers were putting the three children to bed and complaining that it was always in disarray, Liz seemed robotic as she straightened out the blankets.

"What's wrong Liz?" Andrea asked.

Liz looked uncomfortable and responded, "Get the men together for me will you, Andrea? And Dr. Patel too. Willie and I have something to tell everyone."

Willie and Liz emerged together from the safe room. Willie spoke first. "We have an announcement to make, before we get started on our movie tonight." He took a deep breath, and then blurted out, "We think Liz is pregnant again."

Everyone's jaw dropped. Dr. Patel was the first to speak, "Oh my God! Liz!"

"Guys, I am really very sorry. We were taking all precautions to prevent this. I do not know how it happened, I swear!" Liz implored.

Dr. Patel then said, "Babies are wonderful, but when we leave, this one will be so very young."

Liz hung her head. "I know, I know."

Everyone began getting up out of their chairs and pacing around. Then they'd sit, and then they'd jump up again. Colonel Michaels glared at both of them, almost shaking with anger.

The next morning was dark and gloomy. The sun was up but could hardly be seen through the clouds. Colonel Michaels and Dr. Patel were sitting at the table with Willie and Julien, while the other women were outside with the children. The four of them began to discuss the latest pregnancy.

"This has gone too far now," the colonel began. "We need to do something about this pregnancy issue. I swear, I have had enough of this, more than enough! We did not come here to raise a family. Dr. Patel told us years ago that we were not provided with any chemical hormones that would prevent ovulation. Nor do we have the materials to create condoms. What do you two suggest?" he asked as he turned to Willie and Julien.

Both men were dumbfounded. They did not know what to say. All Willie could mumble was that they didn't mean for it to happen.

"This child will be six years old when we depart. The other kids will be 12, 14, and 15. Their survival is precarious. And this new one's survival, well, … cannot be assured …" the colonel trailed off.

Dr. Patel interjected. "I spent last night reviewing my training. When I was in the Indian Military, I was trained on performing vasectomies. I performed one, and I witnessed two others."

Colonel Michaels interrupted, "That makes you an expert."

The little meeting broke up with everyone pondering nervously what Dr. Patel was suggesting.

The following night at dinner, Colonel Michaels addressed the group at the dining table. "The consequences of Liz's pregnancy are iniquitous and cannot be ignored. This baby will be very, very young when we are compelled to leave. Very young indeed. The other children may be too young to care for it. We would be criminally negligent if we allowed the possibility of another pregnancy to occur after this one. I've spoken to Dr. Patel. She assures me that giving Julien and Willie vasectomies would be quick, easy, and almost painless. I think this must be done."

Julien looked at everyone and said, "Painless for her, maybe."

Willie was adamant. "No way. There is no way I'm doing that."

Colonel Michaels' voice sounded firmer than anyone had ever heard before. "We have no choice."

Julien said, "By 'we,' I assume you are going to get one also."

Colonel Michaels responded, "I am not one of the 'we' here. It is not at all necessary for me to get one."

Julien said, "Well, if you don't have to get one, I won't have to get one."

Andrea said, "Stop being a fool, Julien. We do not want our babies to die. Let Arpita do it."

Liz joined in, "She's right, Willie, you've got to do it."

Later that night, Arpita pulled Colonel Michaels into the medical area, half whispering, "Listen, my colonel, you come into the facility and lie on the table for an hour. I'll inject that area with some anesthetic and then you get up and walk around stiff-legged for the rest of the day. Those boys will not inspect you further.

They will assume you were taken care of like they will be."

"Arpita, I never realized you had such a sinister side to you!" the colonel smiled.

The plan worked. Colonel Michaels volunteered to go first. He emerged walking gingerly, pretending to be very sore in this sensitive area.

Using painkillers and local anesthetics while being guided by the computer, Dr. Patel performed vasectomies on the two younger men. They were sore for a day or two, but everyone was very relieved afterwards.

Months later, another baby was born to Liz. It was a girl, and Liz named her Shari, after a running coach she had adored in high school.

Chapter 21

Necessity Is the Constant

TIME REMAINING				
YEARS	***DAYS***	***Hours***	***Minutes***	***Seconds***
6	***70***	***12***	***6***	***18***

Willie and Liz's second child, a pretty baby girl they named Shari, had just been born. Everyone looked at the chronometer with both excitement and worry for the new arrival.

Andrea and Julien were talking. "She will be so young when we leave. We're all wondering if the bigger kids will be able to take care of her," Andrea remarked.

Julien replied, "Well you know, Andrea, after we're gone, these kids are going to grow up and have kids themselves."

"I certainly hope so," declared Andrea. "They are the best part of life. I hope they have normal, happy lives – as best they can, anyway."

"Well, there are two boys and two girls. If each boy takes one girl, that means that Liam is going to have to hook up with his half sister -- or his kids will be hooking up with their cousins," Julien noted.

"Why are you telling me this?" Andrea frowned.

"I'm just thinking aloud, that's all," replied Julien.

"Well, what else can they do? I don't want to talk about that!" Andrea cut the conversation off abruptly.

That evening, Dr. Patel promised to cook a special Indian dessert she had almost forgotten how to make. The guys had recently discovered a beehive in the hollow of a nearby tree, and using smoke to quiet the bees, raided the hive for its honey. The children were amazed at how good it tasted. Honey had not been included as part of the crew's provisions, and so no one had tasted it in years.

"She has him out there wearing a little apron." Denise laughed, remarking on how Dr. Patel always got the colonel to help her cook.

"They make such a cute couple," Andrea commented. "He must be six foot four and she's no taller than five-three. He towers over her, but he follows her around the kitchen like a puppy."

"I think they love each other a lot," smiled Liz warmly. "I wonder, if we had never gone on this journey, would either of them have ever found somebody?"

"I bet he'd have retired from the military as a lonely old soul," Andrea responded.

“And she’d probably have thrown herself into her job as a doctor,” added Denise.

Chapter 22

What Is Unseemly Isn't Always Evil

TIME REMAINING				
YEARS	***DAYS***	***Hours***	***Minutes***	***Seconds***
3	*12*	*20*	*6*	*26*

Little Shari was growing as fast as a weed. And like the other kids, she was happy to learn whatever she could. The other children were very good at watching over her. They didn't let her stumble into thorns or put any strange berries into her mouth. No one could imagine that there had been a time when she was not part of the family. It was as if they had all been together always.

But there were adjustments – not the least of which was one shocking announcement Julien and Willie made after dinner one evening.

"Hey guys," Julien began, getting the attention of the entire crew, "as you know, my specialized expertise has been of little value on this mission. After arrival, I installed 150 yards of P.V.C. pipe between here and the stream, connecting it to our water filtration system. After that, almost nothing more has been required of me. The only other official duty I perform is taking a monthly inventory of supplies. That way, we can return home and tell the people what supplies had not lasted as long as they thought, while they oversupplied us with others."

"So how are we doing?" inquired the colonel.

"Well, we ran out of coffee early, and we are running low on soap" began Julien.

"That's because we are covered in stink and have to shower three times a day," Denise chimed in.

Julien continued, "We are short on soap, running lower than expected on anesthesia, aspirin, and a little behind on salt. But none of that is worrisome. I think if we are a little more careful with these things, they will carry us to the end of our journey. But there is one thing we are really falling behind on. And 'behind' is the operative term here."

"Well, what is it? Spit it out," pressed the colonel.

Julien paused for dramatic effect, and then began, "We were provided 17,000 rolls of toilet paper, but with the creation of all these extra little butts to wipe, our toilet paper supply is running low. At the rate we are using it, we will not have enough to last us until the end of this mission."

"That's terrible!" blurted Andrea.

"But don't worry, a solution is at hand," continued Julien.
"Tell them, Willie," he said, as he handed over the floor to Willie.

Willie stood up, holding something in his hand. "Corn cobs," he said. "Julien and I discussed this problem a few days ago, and we figured that there was no use bringing up a problem unless we also included its solution. We did the research and discovered that primitive people used leaves, stones, and especially corn cobs to wipe themselves. Julien and I have been using them, and we can confirm that one or two corn cobs per 'go' will do an adequate job."

"That is disgusting!" cried Liz.

"I have to use corn cobs to wipe my butt! I don't think I'd have volunteered for this misadventure if I knew I was going to be making fire with sticks, covering my body in vinegar, and wiping my ass with corn cobs," Denise lamented.

"Well," continued Willie, "if you do it in the water, downstream from the intake pipe of course, you use less. The kids will grow corn, and corn cobs are good for everything, from starting a fire to insulating a hut. And there should be plenty of them."

"I think I'm going to be sick," interjected Andrea.

"That's the happy news," continued Julien. "I have something else that might be a little worse."

"Oh no. What could that be?" Denise inquired with a worried frown.

"Kristina is getting older. She will soon have to address the menstrual problem; and Shari will eventually have to as well. Willie and I researched this too and found out that primitive females used strips of beaver hide, squirrel tails, or deer fur. They can be boiled clean and used one time or boiled and used again," Julien replied, with firm authority.

"Besides, we have no choice." he continued.

As if paralyzed by the thought, Liz, Andrea, and Denise all held their heads in their hands as they wondered how they were going to set this example for their little girls.

Dr. Patel looked over at the colonel and remarked, "I was never so happy as now to have gone through menopause and not have to face this problem."

Chapter 23

The Departure

TIME REMAINING				
YEARS	***DAYS***	***Hours***	***Minutes***	***Seconds***
0	***21***	***5***	***47***	***11***

Colonel Michaels, growing a little grey with the passing of time, was frequently found alone in the kitchen, rocking back on a chair, looking like he was feeling the weight of his many years of responsibility. As the time to depart approached, the thought of leaving the children and the happy life the group had made for itself was grim. Thinking about it made his chest hurt, and he finally understood where the expression, *my heart is breaking,* came from.

Every adult could occasionally be found doing something similar. Sometimes sitting, sometimes standing, staring blankly at nothing in particular; everyone doing their best to recall every second of the life that was soon to be no more.

The arrival of the children had an unexpected and insidious effect on everyone's enthusiasm for the mission. The children, and not our lost humanity, became the focus of everyone's existence. Years ago, Julien and Willie had been sent on a number of scouting missions in various directions.

Each took them hundreds of miles, north, south, east, and west. But every expedition turned up nothing. Eventually, further scouting seemed pointless, and the practice was given up.

In the last few years of their mission, there had been little thought, and even less effort invested in discovering what had happened to people. Whatever it was had occurred long ago, and this group was not going to figure it out, not at this location anyway. Now in its final days, that assignment was coming to an end, and no one cared much about its failure. All the crew could think about, and weep about, was leaving the children and the serene life they had made for themselves. They had enjoyed the entire earth all to themselves, and it had come to feel like paradise.

Raising the children and working hard to learn the skills of primitive survival had transformed them.

From the time he was a young cadet in the Marine Academy, the colonel had pondered life's "big questions": *What am I on this earth for? What's it all about? What is the meaning of life?* He was now convinced that he had discovered the answers to those questions on this mission. The meaning of life was found in focusing on the things that give life its meaning. The meaning of a shoe is found in its relation to the foot it protects; the meaning of a chair lies in its connection to supporting the people who sit on it.

So, the *meaning* of anything is discovered through its relationship to the other things around it. The meaning of our lives is found in our relationships with the other lives around us. Without those other lives, our life would really have little meaning. And the more we are involved with others, the more meaning our life, and their lives, gain. We *mean* something to them, and they *mean* something to us.

In their final days, the silence of any quiet room invited these melancholy reflections of tenderness; feelings that often became overwhelming. There was such a dichotomy now between the lives of the children and that of the adults. The children were always happy, playing, laughing, and going about their lives completely undisturbed and unaware of how things were about to change; while the adults grew increasingly unhappy, disturbed, sullen, tearful and reflective in anticipation of the change that was soon to take them away from everything they valued most.

As the day of departure neared, the crew grew increasingly morose. Sixteen years ago, they had imagined the approach of their return would be a most joyful and exciting time. They looked forward to being antsy and anxious, impatient to return home and become rich and famous. But none of that mattered at all now. This future world had become their *Garden of Eden*, even if it did contain the occasional snake, ants or bees. And now they were leaving it, being "kicked out of it" as it were, this time by an unbending God called *the laws of physics.*

In the final weeks, every adult had gotten into the habit of leaving the others and walking alone through the woods, out of sight. There they would shed unseen tears. The colonel had begun a nightly ritual of going through his copious notes to find and recall little anecdotes about the children. It was not unusual for him to emerge from his room with another story about something one of the kids had said or done from years past.

"Hey, you guys remember this?" asked the colonel, walking from his room. "It was when Liam was four years old, and Liz was telling him about Santa Claus. She told him how Santa comes when everyone is sleeping to leave them gifts. Then Liz asked him, 'Would you like to meet Santa?' and Liam shook his head, *no*. When Liz inquired why not, Liam, with a worried look on his face, turned to his mother and asked, '*Where are his* claws'*?*"

Everyone laughed recalling the memory.

The colonel dug up another memory the following night. "Recall when Andrea was telling Kristina one of her Bible stories. Kristina must have been about five. Andrea told her the story of Lot and his daughters, and how angels had told him to take his possessions and flee, and to go off into the desert. At the end of the story, Andrea asked Kristina if she liked it. But little Kristina looked troubled and asked, '*What happened to their flea!?*'"

On another occasion, the colonel reminded the group about the day he had gotten back from an outing that had taken him away from the compound for a couple of days. When he returned, little Stephen said to him, "Colonel Michaels, sometimes, when you are away, I forget you exist!"

Everyone would laugh at the colonel's retellings, leading to a sniffle here or there. It was as if they wanted to soak up every memory, so as not to forget a thing. It was a sort of sentimental torture for grieving souls, a grim and gloomy happiness that they could not get enough of.

People tend to recall the most salient and meaningful experiences of their past, those that left the strongest impression on them at the time. Often those experiences are "firsts": their first day at school, their first crush, their first date,

the first time they flew in an airplane, the first time they were hospitalized, the first time their child pulled himself up to a standing position or addressed them as
"Mommy" or "Daddy."

Fortunately, under most circumstances, the realities of life spare us from the knowledge of our very "lasts." Generally speaking, we do not know an experience we are having is going to be the last one of its kind: we do not know that this is the last time we hold our child's hand crossing the street, or the last time we will ever speak to our grandmother.

But they were not being spared these realizations. They all knew the very moment that would be the *last time* they would ever see their children, the *last time* they would hold their child's little hand, and the *last time* they would ever give them a kiss. The pain seemed too much for a human heart to bear.

Chapter 24

An Amazing Discovery

TIME REMAINING				
YEARS	***DAYS***	***Hours***	***Minutes***	***Seconds***
0	***16***	***11***	***13***	***11***

From her bedroom, Denise called out to whoever was in the kitchen, “Can you see the kids?”

Liz, glancing at the monitor, responded with a smile. “Yup, they’re all playing by the sliding stone. They’ve really made that thing huge. It started out being about only six feet long, and now it is at least fifteen feet long! The rain has made gullies along each side of it.”

Denise walked into the kitchen, chuckling. “I think it’s more like 20 feet long! They keep sliding down it, clearing away more dirt and weeds and uncovering more of the rock. It’s getting so long now that they get up quite a bit of speed going down. Shari is too small; she still won’t do it. She’s afraid.”

“She’ll be doing it before too long,” Liz assured her. “Where’s Andrea?” she asked.

Denise sighed as she turned from the monitor. "She's in her room. We'll be leaving in only a handful of days, and I think it's really getting to her. She is having a tough time coming to terms with it. I am, too."

Her voice slightly cracked as she continued, "I try not to think about it. Every time I see any of the kids, I just want to grab them, kiss them, and squeeze them tight. The kids think I'm going crazy. I am. I can't think about it," Denise lamented as she turned her head slightly away.

Suddenly, Liam ran in, breathless and flushed, sweaty and in need of a drink. Liz turned to him with a smile. "Liam, what are you kids doing? Stop running around and take a break. Did you all sleep well in the huts you made up on the hill?"

"Yes, we slept okay," he replied, gulping down water. "But we all wanted to come back here and sleep in the house."

Liz's expression grew serious. "Well, the men say you have to spend another night in your huts, and beginning tonight, you have to spend two nights in a row in your huts and then one night back here."

Liam rolled his eyes. "I think they just like to torture us kids."

"They are doing it for your own good. What are you doing outside now?" his mother asked.

"Playing ***Timenell***," Liam answered, his voice filled with the excitement of childhood.

"Playing what?" Liz asked, completely taken aback.

"Playing *Timenell*," Liam repeated. "It's a game where the smaller kids chase me, and I have to slide down the sliding stone to get away."

Liz's eyes widened. "I haven't heard that funny name in sixteen years. Did Colonel Michaels teach you that game? Did he tell you to call it that name?"

Liam shook his head. "No. It's written on the sliding stone, so that's what we call it now."

Denise, who had been listening intently, frowned. "What's written on the sliding stone?"

"*Timenell,*" Liam replied simply.

"Did you write it there, or did one of the men write it?" Denise pressed.

"No. We just uncovered the carving this morning. It's carved deep into the stone. It was hidden under all the weeds. We were clearing them out to make the sliding stone even longer, and we came across the word, *'Timenell'* with an arrow."

Denise's face paled. "Oh my God! Liz, find the guys. Tell them to meet us at the sliding stone."

The entire crew was alerted, and everyone raced up the hill to the sliding stone. Colonel Michaels saw the carving and immediately instructed Willie and Julien to run back to the compound and get picks and shovels. "We have to dig this thing out."

The men soon uncovered the complete engraving with an arrow pointing to a box-like shape at the base of the structure. "Apparently, they, the people from the past, want us to break this thing open," Colonel Michaels mused aloud. "There must be something in here for us – probably contraceptives that actually work!"

"It's a little late for that," mumbled Andrea.

They started to dig with dogged determination all around the huge stone. Julien's eyes widened in recognition as they worked. "It's a giant obelisk. It must have been constructed here on the hill overlooking the compound so that we'd be sure to see it when we arrived. But it apparently must have fallen over sometime during the 9,000 years since it was built. There must have been a few earthquakes in all that time. I wonder what they were trying to send us? More supplies, maybe?"

The crew retrieved sledgehammers to smash open the concrete at the bottom of the structure. Inside was a chamber with a large metal box. The box had deteriorated badly. Using a four- wheeler, they carried it carefully down to the compound and pulled its pieces apart.

Inside were four smaller compartments. Each had been meticulously filled with something, probably a sort of packing material. One contained deteriorated parchment made from leather; another appeared to be oxidized metal plates; the third held pieces of slate, now broken to bits; and the fourth contained some severely corroded computer disks and thumb drives.

It was clear that whoever had built this huge structure was trying to send a message to the crew. Now it was up to them to decipher what it was. And they didn't have much time to do it.

Chapter 25

One Last Challenge

TIME REMAINING				
YEARS	*DAYS*	*Hours*	*Minutes*	*Seconds*
0	*13*	*5*	*47*	*00*

Denise stood over the crumbling remains of the boxes, her face etched in frustration. "These four boxes contain something, but it has all deteriorated. And it looks like much of it has been consumed by bacteria or oxidized to dust."

Colonel Michaels nodded, "This giant obelisk was built on the hill overlooking our compound. They put it here thinking we could never miss it. Whatever these things are telling us, they've been inside this monstrosity for 9000 years. They must have thought it was mighty important. Can anything really last that long?"

"We'll have to bring everything into the laboratory and try to examine it piece-by-piece, in regular and ultraviolet light, even using X-rays," Denise suggested. "But it is important that we do not disturb them too much. Everything looks like it is falling apart, crumbling away."

Andrea, who had been quietly contemplating the situation, spoke up. "What of the computer drives? Is it possible that they could be readable after ninety centuries?"

Colonel Michaels turned to Julien. "Julien, help the women move this equipment around. Let's get started trying to figure out what they were trying to tell us. I wish we had found this stuff 16 years ago. Now we have only a few days to decipher it."

Julien nodded, a determined look on his face. "I'm just glad we found it now. If it weren't for the kids, we'd have never found it."

That evening at dinner, Colonel Michaels addressed the crew: "The people of the past have tried to send us some sort of message. Our task consists of trying to decipher it. Let's not get distracted from that."

Days passed and it was determined that nothing could be made out of the computer disks, thumb drives, and parchment. All they could do was try to put together something from the remains of the metal plates and the slate.

Six more days passed before the colonel announced that the jigsaw puzzle was finally coming together. "By tomorrow, we should know what they were trying to tell us."

In the medical area, Colonel Michaels addressed Denise, Julien, and Andrea. "Luckily, I had some code-breaking training in the military. These bits and pieces of slate that you are funneling over to me are like a coded crossword puzzle. But some things are falling into place now. As best I can figure out, the parchment, slate, and metal plates were all saying the same thing. They must have put the exact same message on the four different formats, not knowing what might survive."

Denise, perplexed, wondered out loud, "What could possibly be so important that they could go to all this trouble setting up this monument?"

Colonel Michaels sighed. "They carved the messages onto pieces of slate. Those should have survived. But whatever caused the obelisk to topple over—probably an earthquake—shattered the slate into a thousand pieces. Over the course of 9000 years, there must have been a few more quakes, each jumbling the carved slate.

The following afternoon, Colonel Michaels walked out of the medical area, stiff and achy from having worked tirelessly on deciphering the message for the past 24 hours. He looked astonished. He called the group together with an odd tone in his voice. "It has taken much of the time we have remaining to put enough of the pieces together to allow me to figure out the communication. When I did, I could hardly believe what I was reading and thought it was ludicrous. But after checking and rechecking, the information is clear, and it is as abysmal as it is unambiguous." He paused, as if the very words refused to leave his mouth.

"As I told you all at breakfast, I was on the verge of figuring out enough of the message to soon determine its contents. After reading it, I have to conclude that it was a stroke of luck that we found it, an act of God maybe. And possibly a bigger stroke of luck that we didn't find it earlier. In fact, I suppose we found it at about the best time we could."

Willie looked confused. "I don't get it, Colonel."

Colonel Michaels continued, his voice steady but somber. "Recall that this is from the past. The people who made this obelisk knew us. They knew us, and they created this AFTER we had returned from the future. Apparently, we went back, and we were celebrated as heroes at first. We were sent on a worldwide tour visiting nations in every part of the globe. We were acclaimed everywhere. Then something began to happen. It is unclear to me how it happened. Too much of the message is missing. But evidently, after we went back, they were able to determine why we were never able to find people here. We never figured it out, but they did, after we came back."

Willie's eyes widened in disbelief. "After we got back, they figured it out after all? So, what happened? What happened to all the people?"

"We killed them. *Timenell* killed them," Colonel Michaels said, the words hanging heavily in the air.

Julien was stunned. "Huh! What does that mean, 'we killed them'? How did we kill them?"

Colonel Michaels explained. "Apparently, we went back in time, and we brought back with us a virus of some sort. Whatever the virus or microbe was, it was turned on or amplified by time travel. We contracted it in the future, but it did not affect us here. It only became virulent after our return."

"That is remarkable!" Dr. Patel blurted out.

"Shortly after our return, after our tour around the world" the colonel continued, "everyone on earth began to contract some terrible illness and died rapidly. There was no cure ever found. They never even figured out how it was transmitted from one person to the next. But by the time the scientists had figured out that it was a virus that came back with us, there was hardly any time, or any trained people left, to do much research. And they were lucky to find the workers to build this obelisk."

Julien shook his head, trying to comprehend the gravity of the situation. "What were they trying to tell us? What can we do?
We don't have any viruses. We're not sick."

"The message that was sent to us was that mankind was becoming extinct. All mankind apparently became extinct, or was going extinct, a few years after we returned. At least they were, at the time they made this obelisk. They imagined they had little time left. Apparently, they all died because of us; because of something we brought back with us," Colonel Michaels continued.

Dr. Patel, her voice trembling, was dumbfounded. "This is too utterly fantastic to be true. Can it really be true?"

Colonel Michaels nodded solemnly. "We haven't been able to find any traces of humanity because everyone died 9000 years ago, shortly after we returned to the 21st century. Even us, I suppose. We die shortly after we return. We die with everyone else."

Andrea spoke up. "Maybe it's nature's way of keeping time travel from happening. Nature kills off all the time travelers."

Dr. Patel was incredulous. "Wow! All humans extinct. I was expecting to go back to a hero's welcome. Now, I'm going to go back to a graveyard. We're leaving one empty world to go back to another."

Colonel Michaels corrected her gently. "No, Arpita. When we go back, they will all still be there. We will go back to a world full of people – of happy people who are not yet aware of the destruction that is about to befall them. But shortly after we get back, the end will come. We will bring death to our people. That is what the message is all about. There is a lot more than that written on the slate, something about the results of what little research they were able to carry out before the end. But I can't make it out."

"Well, now that we know this, when we go back, the minute we get back, we can tell everyone about this, and they can get busy working on the cure as soon as we return," Willie blurted out enthusiastically.

The colonel cleared his throat and continued, "The slate tells us to research the virus. They expected us to have 16 years to do the research and discover the problem and its solution. Presumably, they included an electron microscope in with these items, but it was so disintegrated we couldn't even recognize it was here."

"And the story gets worse," he went on. "They also tell us that no matter what, we must not bring this pathogen back with us. They even go so far as to tell us in no uncertain terms how to avoid bringing this disease back to them. It tells us what we must do to save humanity."

Dr. Patel, her voice rising shrill and almost in a panic, asked, "What must we do? What can we do? I know that tone in your voice; something is very wrong. What are they telling us to do?"

Colonel Michaels took a deep breath, steeling himself for the hardest part. "We were sent here to figure out how to save humanity. Saving humanity has always been our mission, and it is still our mission. I don't know how to tell you all this, but we must not go back. We can only save humanity by not going back."

Julien was astonished. "That's fine with me… but we have to go back. We can't help it, and we'll go back whether we want to or not. That's what they always said. None of us wants to go back, but we all have to."

Colonel Michaels shook his head. "The message is unmistakable. It says that we cannot go back alive. These messages we've deciphered tell us that we have to be sure we destroy ourselves before we go back. We must do it for mankind."

Andrea's voice trembled as she frowned, "What do they mean, 'destroy ourselves'?"

Colonel Michaels continued. "Included in the message are instructions. These instructions are pretty simple. Julien can follow them, and I think I could even follow them. We all have to follow them."

Andrea, her face growing pale, asked again, "What do they mean 'destroy ourselves,' what do the instructions say? What are we supposed to do?"

Colonel Michaels straightened himself up, and spoke in a halting manner, as if he could hardly believe what he was saying. "We volunteered for this mission to find out what happened to humanity. Now, it is our job to save it."

Denise, her patience wearing thin, demanded, "Save it how? Stop beating around the bush and tell us what you mean."

Colonel Michaels began, "These instructions are 9000 years old, but they are clear. They instruct us to divert the energy from the nuclear-generating electrical system to the walls of the safe room. Once diverted, we are to rig it so that we can flip a switch from inside the room, and the walls will heat up to a red-hot condition. The safe room consists of two layers of inch-thick steel. The inner layer, where we will be, will heat up to over 1800 degrees. We will be inside it.

Essentially, we are being told we must become pieces of toast in a toaster. We will be cremated. What will return to the past in about three days from now will only be our ashes. Any virus within us will be destroyed, and humankind will be saved. Neither we nor the virus will survive our cremation. They figured out that much."

All the color left Liz's face. "That is horrible. I won't do it. I'm not going to kill myself. First, you tell me that I have to leave my children. Now you say I have to kill myself. It's too much to ask any mother."

The colonel repeated the final command they had received from the past. "We must be reduced to ashes. Even the tiniest portion of our bodies not being cremated will certainly bring the virus back to humanity."

After the colonel broke the news, everyone retreated to their rooms. Liz and Willie went to one room and closed the door; Denise, Andrea, and Julien to another; and Dr. Patel and the Colonel to her room. They were all stunned, trying to absorb the impact of this final and most horrible of all traumas.

The next morning found the children laughing and playing outside, blissfully unaware of the impending doom that loomed over their parents. The adults used to cry about the separation that was at hand; now that separation seemed their smaller concern. Their very deaths were now only a couple of days away.

Slowly, each person came to recognize that they had no choice. To save humanity, they had to destroy themselves. Knowing the hour of one's own death – a death coming at one's own hands – was the ultimate torment. Their minds found it all incomprehensible.

They couldn't help but hold and hug the children and even embrace each other as they passed in the halls. It was as if they were already deceased, still walking around, but dead inside. When there is no tomorrow, today doesn't matter much either. They were all condemned, everyone looking up at the chronometer a hundred times an hour, counting the remaining minutes of their existence.

Chapter 26

What Is Courage?

TIME REMAINING				
YEARS	*DAYS*	*Hours*	*Minutes*	*Seconds*
0	*2*	*9*	*3*	*15*

Julien Bernard was sweating as he labored to pull the electrical cable from the nuclear reactor to the steel walls of the safe room. “I never in a thousand years thought I’d be constructing my own death chamber. Now I’m glad I read the Koran, anyway,” he said to Colonel Michaels as he entered the room.

“I’ve done a lot of reading, but not much on eschatology,” said the colonel.

“What’s eschatology?” asked Julien.

“It’s the investigation into the afterlife – what may or may not happen after death,” answered the colonel.

“Heaven is made to sound great,” said Julien. “But I notice no one is ever in a rush to get there.”

The thought of their deaths had taken on an unreal aspect. They could talk about it as if it were something that would only happen in theory – or only to somebody else.

"Well," began the colonel, "it is like Marcus Aurelius noted twenty-five hundred years ago … well, over 11,000 years ago now, I suppose. Death is either the termination of sensation, in which case there is nothing to really worry about; or it is a different sort of existence, in which case we don't really die, but live some other sort of life."

After a short pause, the colonel asked, "Do you need my help here?"

Julien shook his head, "No, this wiring is simple enough. We'll rig it to be switched on from inside the safe room. We go in, lock the door, flip the switch, and with this much power being applied, we should begin to fry in less than a minute. The process of reducing everyone completely to ashes will take about two hours. Flip that switch, and there is no turning back. Flip that switch, and we'll all be dead in minutes, and within two hours, only ashes will remain. That should do it."

Colonel Michaels let out a sigh. "Being burned alive is no way to go. Don't mention this to the others. Just act as if it will all be quick and painless."

He walked past Denise and Andrea sitting at the kitchen table, both staring zombie-like into space.

The colonel found the doctor and grabbed her by the arm. "Arpita, listen. What we have to do is horrific. But we can't cook ourselves alive. No one has that kind of courage. We'll all chicken out at the end. I feel like I want to chicken out now. It's too gruesome. Isn't there some type of sedative you can give us, to put us all to sleep first?"

Dr. Patel nodded slowly. "Yes, of course. But no sedative that I have will keep you asleep under those conditions. Feeling that level of pain will wake us up. We are all going to die horrible, painful deaths. Being conscious while we burn to death is the worst possible way to die. I can't even think about it."

"Well, that's what I mean," continued the colonel. "That's what I want to avoid. Can't you rig up a sedative so powerful that it will keep us unconscious through the heat?"

Dr. Patel shook her head. "No. None of the sedatives I have can do that – not unless they are given in lethal doses. We've been provided potentially lethal anesthesia in case some serious operation needed to be performed. But we were not expected to need much of it. I have some. If given in large enough doses, it will kill, that is certain. I can make a sedative strong enough to kill everyone peacefully using that. It's better than burning. But anything short of a lethal dose and you will surely wake up and feel the fire."

Colonel Michaels nodded and took a deep breath. "Well, that's it then. That is what needs to be done. You need to prepare enough anesthesia to inject each of us with a lethal dose. We will die sleeping rather than burning. There is no other possible choice.

You must do this for the rest of us. You inject everybody. I'll be last. I'll flip the switch and then inject myself. Then we will all be gone."

Dr. Patel choked up and could hardly speak. "I am sorry, my Colonel. I will not do it. I will not kill my friends. You are all my family now. I cannot hurt them. I will never be able to do it. You cannot expect this from me. I will let you inject me, but I will never inject you."

That night, Colonel Michaels lay in his bed unable to fall asleep, thinking about how he and Arpita had gone back and forth all day discussing the plan. They finally agreed that Arpita would assemble a different hypodermic needle for each crew member – each filled with a lethal dose of the sedative – and that he would inject everyone with a dose large enough not only to put them to sleep but to kill them quickly.

"I hope I have the courage to do it," he thought to himself. He was convinced that he was doing the right thing, doing his family a favor by sparing them pain. He recalled Aristotle's observation that ***of all the virtues, 'courage' was the most important because without courage, none of the other virtues could be realized.*** Now he understood what the greatest of all philosophers had meant.

His mind frequently jumped from philosophy to poetry, as it searched for a way to make sense of it all. On how to come to terms with his own death, and of how to face the dissolute emptiness of never hearing the children's laughter again.

Sometimes he was reminded of the line from Edgar Allan Poe's famous poem of everlasting loss:

'*Quoth the Raven, nevermore.*'

But more often it was Shakespeare's most depressing of all sonnets that returned to his mind. The sonnet of man's greatest enemy, and the only adversary that can never be defeated: *Time.*

If this mission had taught him anything, it had demonstrated how '*time*' must inexorably wipe away all vestiges of man's proud accomplishments. Where before there was everything, there must eventually be nothing. And how cruel time was, wiping away his own life and his own loves. That the most important things in his life will soon be gone forever.

He watched his friends sob as they kissed their children. He recognized that they were not thinking of the happiness that they held in their arms today, but in the sadness of its certain loss tomorrow.

And though the great bard's poem had been written over 9000 years before, Sonnet 64 seemed composed especially for them:

When I have seen by Time's fell hand defaced
The rich proud cost of outworn buried age;
When lofty towers I see down-razed
And brass eternal slave to mortal rage;
Ruin hath taught me thus to ruminate,
That Time will come and take my love away.

This thought is as a death, which cannot choose
But weep to have that which it fears to lose.

The colonel came to understand how poetry and philosophy were two different, but complimentary, methods used to resolve, and finally to accept, the ineffably poignant realities of our mortality.

Taking a deep breath, he tried to put aside his contemplation.

He went over his plan a hundred times in his mind. “We’ll tell everyone that it is only a strong sedative. We won’t let them know that the injection is lethal. We’ll tell them that it is going to make them sleep. Then, after injecting the others, I will pull the switch that begins the destruction, and then I will finally inject myself.”

The last two days passed like a slow-moving funeral. Everyone spent as much time as they could with each child. Everyone had reviewed all the skills that had been passed on to them. Everyone had said, “I love you,” a thousand times.

Their final moments together were approaching.

Chapter 27

The Ultimate Complication

TIME REMAINING				
YEARS	***DAYS***	***Hours***	***Minutes***	***Seconds***
0	***1***	***3***	***32***	***56***

The day before they would be forced to do the awful deed, Dr. Patel rushed over to the colonel and said, "Kevin, I have to talk to you."

Colonel Michaels knew it had to be serious by the tone of her voice. She had almost never called him by his first name before. They hurried back into the medical area where it appeared Dr. Patel was nervously shaking with anxiety.

"What is it, Arpita? How bad can it be?" asked the colonel.

"I think we are already facing the worst."

"Not quite the worst, my love. I have to tell you the worst," she said.

"Well, what is it?" asked the colonel.

"It's the anesthesia. I have to measure it out by weight. And if I give everyone the same size dose for their body size, there will not be enough to ensure everyone's death. They will go to sleep for a while, but they will not die. They will probably wake up when the heat comes."

"That's horrible. I can't believe it! Is friggin' God himself against us?!?" the colonel asked angrily.

Pausing for a moment, his tone grew quiet. "You have to administer this drug by weight. And I am by far the biggest and heaviest here. I will require the most. If I were not to get a shot, it would leave a good amount for the rest. If I did not take an injection, would there be enough for the others?" the colonel inquired stoically.

The doctor couldn't get herself to say it out l"ud, but she nodded her head.

Staring off into space for a moment, then gathering himself, the colonel replied, "Well, that's it then. We won't tell the others, we'll let them go on believing that I will take an injection like the rest of them. Be sure to mark everyone's hypodermic needle clearly. Mine will contain only water."

Dr. Patel began to cry as she hugged the man she had grown to love and the man who deeply loved her.

"Come on now," said the colonel. "I'm an officer in the Marine Corps after all. And a philosopher to boot. As a Marine, you know that you may be asked to die for your country at any time. And someone once described philosophy as little more than a long preparation for death. Let's you and I act like there is nothing wrong. The others are looking to us for leadership today and tomorrow, more than ever."

On the morning of their final day, Denise fought back tears as she hugged the children, "All you kids go up by the sliding stone and watch. You will be amazed. This entire building will disappear, and we will be gone. But you will have to stay there for a long time. Don't come back down."

Andrea, openly crying, hugged the children. "You guys remember to be good. Remember to think of us and that we will always be with you. Remember all the things we taught you. When it gets dark, go into your huts. Tomorrow, Liam will lead you all."

Shari asked, "But where are you going, mommy? I want to go with you."

Andrea replied, "You can't go with mommy, baby. Go up the hill with the other kids. Liam, Stevie, and Kristina will take care of you. You will sleep in the big huts we've made, and the boys will hunt and fish. Just remember to pray, and mommy will hear you. Mommy will always be watching over you."

Liz hugged Liam tightly. "Liam, you are the big man now. You have to take care of all the children. I know that you can do everything. You are so smart. Remember us always. Come back to the sliding stone every now and then, if you can, and try to remember us. Try to remember what we looked like and sounded like. And keep all the kids up there until we are gone." She broke down in tears as she pulled herself away.

The men gave all the children hugs, and Colonel Michaels led the children to the base of the hill. "You kids go up to the sliding stone and stay there. Don't come down. Liam, be sure to keep them all up there."

The colonel turned to Willie. "Okay, Willie, have Liam take all the kids up the hill and have them sit on the sliding stone. Goodbye, Liam. Goodbye, kids. You are about to see something you will hardly believe. We have to go back now to the place we came from – far away. Don't come off this hill until tomorrow."

Willie walked part way up the hill and stopped, saying, "Take all the kids the rest of the way up the hill, Liam. I love you."

Liam, still confused, asked, "I still don't understand. Where are you going?"

Willie replied, "We're going back to the place we came from. I can't explain it, but in some ways, it's very, very far away. We knew we could only stay for a while. We were sent here only to stay a short time. We always knew we had to go back. We created you here, and you have to stay here. We were created in another place."

Liam shrugged, resigned, and said, "I just don't understand. Okay, alright. Goodbye. Goodbye, everybody. I don't believe you are going anywhere but I'll do as you ask."

With the children assembled on the hill, the group moved inside and toward the safe room. Everyone knew it was the walk of the condemned. It was a walk of death. Once inside that room, they would never step out again.

"It's time," Colonel Michaels said. "Less than three hours left, let's go in."

They all glanced at the chronometer as they entered, as if to record the time of their own demise.

TIME REMAINING				
YEARS	***DAYS***	***Hours***	***Minutes***	***Seconds***
0	***0***	***2***	***59***	***6***

Each person stepped through the door and sat down upon the individual cot that had been made for them to lie upon. As Liz was about to cross the threshold, she began to shake. She paused, and then she panicked.

"No! No! I won't do this. I can't do it!" Liz held onto the doorway and refused to go in.

"Take hold of her, Willie. Get her inside," Colonel Michaels commanded.

"No! I won't do it, let me go! Please," Liz screamed, throwing her hands up and grabbing the door frame, holding on as tightly as she could.

Willie had never before refused to listen to Liz when she was adamant about something. But this time he stiffened his resolve, put his hands around her waist and yanked her through the doorway onto her cot. She fell down there, throwing her head onto his shoulder, sobbing.

"Arpita, help Willie calm her down," Colonel Michaels asked.

Dr. Patel sat there holding Liz's hand and addressed the group. "Everyone, lie down on your own cot. We went over this, many times. Lie down and stretch out your arm. Nothing is going to hurt you."

"Everyone, lie on your own cot as we discussed," Colonel Michaels repeated.

Julien, stretching out his arm, said, "Okay chief, I'll go first. Give me the shot."

Colonel Michaels walked over, fighting the tears that were welling up in his eyes, and gave his lifelong companion the injection. "Well, it doesn't hurt," Julien smirked.

"Goodnight, my friend," said the colonel as he patted Julien on the shoulder.

"Just close your eyes and you'll fall asleep," Dr. Patel whispered from the cot next to him.

Colonel Michaels then went and gave each person their own injection. "Goodbye, Willie. Goodbye, Liz. Goodbye, Denise. Goodbye, Andrea," he said to each one, in a whisper. They all became quiet and closed their eyes. The colonel turned finally to Arpita.

"I have to be the one to secure the door and flip on the heating switch. After it is flipped, it will quickly be over. We'll all meet again in the next world, I'm sure of it," he said.

Liz, mumbling while slipping into unconsciousness, "I want to meet again in this world. This world has become like Heaven to me. I want to come back to the children, and I want…" her voice got softer and trailed off.

A minute later, Dr. Patel went around to each cot and confirmed everyone was dead. She then went to her cot, where she and the colonel sat for a moment holding hands and looking into each other's eyes. They gave each other one final kiss goodbye.

She reached into a pocket and pulled out a handful of pills. "These are strong pain killers," she said. "They may make things easier. I brought a glass of water for you too."

The colonel took them from her and made one last little joke.

"I hope these are not habit forming. Besides, I'll need all my wits about me to pull this off. I won't swallow them until I'm sure everything is going off correctly."

"Goodbye, my Colonel, my love. I am off to see my little Jahnvi. Jahnvi and I will be waiting for you," Dr. Patel said, tearing up. She slowly lay down on her cot and closed her eyes. Colonel Michaels, wiping the tears from his own eyes, gave her the injection and said, "Goodbye, my love."

Colonel Michaels took one last look at the clock.

TIME REMAINING				
YEARS	***DAYS***	***Hours***	***Minutes***	***Seconds***
0	***0***	***2***	***39***	***49***

The children were all assembled on the sliding stone. The colonel locked the door to the safe room and looked over at all the cots. Every member of the crew looked peacefully asleep; he knew they were all dead.

He inhaled deeply, his last thoughts going back to his own parents and his own childhood; of the day he graduated from the academy, and of the very first time he looked out of the door of the compound and into this uninhabited world. He gathered these thoughts together and reflected that people had been right, that before you die, your life seems to flash before your eyes.

Up on the hill, Kristina looked down on the compound.

"Nothing is happening!"

Shari complained, "I'm hungry. This is boring! I want to go back to the house and get something to eat. I don't want to stay out here in these stupid huts." She started to get up and walk down the hill toward the house. Liam got up and grabbed her arm.

"Just wait. They told us to sit here, and we will see something. They told us not to move from this spot until the house disappears," Liam said firmly.

Stevie added, "I don't think anything is going to happen. I don't want the house to disappear. I don't want to stay out here in these huts either."

"We have no choice. We will never have a choice again," Liam told them firmly.

Inside, as the last person alive, Colonel Michaels said one last prayer to a God he hoped existed and to one he hoped would have mercy on him. He took another deep breath, checked the door to be sure it was locked, and then flipped on the heat switch and sat down on his cot.

"Hey, I better check the walls to be sure they are heating up. If something is wrong, I'll have to fix it," he thought to himself. Standing up and stepping forward, he reached out and touched the wall. It burned his hand so severely that his skin sizzled. It was so painfully hot that he jumped back, dropping the pills on the floor. The room was rapidly getting so blisteringly hot that he couldn't see or even think straight. The soles of his shoes were beginning to melt, and sweat was pouring off of his head. His final thoughts were that of perdition. Maybe he was being forced to pay the penalty for killing his friends. Maybe he was being made to feel the fires of Hell.

Outside, the children could almost make out the screams of the colonel as he felt the liquid in his own eyes boiling. He fell down, conscious only long enough to hear the skin on his face sizzle as it contacted the floor. He fried to death in his own skin.

Two hours later, and minutes before the compound blinked back to the past, the heat automatically shut off.

Chapter 28

Where the Future Becomes the Past

Oct. 7, 2058

Back in the year 2058, the people of the past were assembled, nervously awaiting the return of the time travelers. An unnerving, though not totally unanticipated problem loomed, one that threatened the launch of the next mission, **Timenell 2**.

Located 75 miles east of the initial *Timenell* mission, the second mission was located only 12 miles inland from the Georgia seacoast. Disconcertingly, an extremely large Category 4 hurricane was scheduled to make landfall and pass directly over *Timenell 2's* location in less than 8 hours. The planners had known that this location was risky, and for this very reason, but had decided years before to go ahead with a launch from this site as it was considered an area "very likely" to be inhabited.

The problem was that the fantastic amount of energy needed to propel the next mission into the future might be jeopardized by power fluctuations caused by the strong winds of a hurricane. But the mission had been planned, manned, and paid for, and it was too late to change venues now. Years of effort would not be thrown away unless the launch proved beyond a doubt to be too dangerous.

It was decided that the *Timenell* reception ground crew, waiting for the first manned mission to return, would remain on the phone, in constant contact with the technicians and leaders in charge of the second mission. And, as soon as the first mission blinked back safely, the second mission would be given the green light to launch -- avoiding the hurricane by only a few hours.

The compound carrying the remains of the crew blinked back to the year 2058, just as the theoretical physicists predicted it would. All gasped as the huge facility simply reappeared. The old leadership team led by General Yadev had long since retired. The team was now commanded by Debra Ivanov, recently promoted to the rank of General, along with her second-in-command, Colonel Kaddour.

Colonel Kaddour was a representative of the government of Pakistan and had only recently been brought onto the *Timenell* staff. He was particularly excited by the return of the time travelers and was instructed to remain on the phone with the people overseeing the *Timenell 2* mission.

He was told that as soon as the giant facility reappeared, he was to inform them, so that they could decide when to send forward the next mission. Once he saw the enormous facility reappear, he happily reported, "Okay, the compound has returned and looks fine."

With that he ended the phone call, confident that everything would be well. He could never have foreseen what he and his superior, General Ivanov, were about to discover.

Turning to the general, Colonel Kaddour said, “Okay, General, I told them. I expect them to send forward their crew soon, ahead of the storm.”

“This must be a happy day for you, General,” Colonel Kaddour went on. “I understand that you were part of the original team that sent these people ahead in time 16 years ago.”

General Ivanov nodded and could not help but grin, “You told them the *Timenell* crew were back?”

“Yes I did,” confirmed the colonel.

“That’s a relief,” sighed General Ivanov.

She was looking forward to meeting her old colleagues and could not wait to be briefed on their experiences. She beamed as she said, “Yes, we sent them off a long time ago. I thought this day would never come. I can’t begin to describe the feeling of excitement surrounding their send-off; it’s only exceeded by the thrill of having them come back. The Kremlin, the White House, and the rest of the world are standing by, waiting for my call confirming their safe arrival and the successful departure of the next mission. I’ll get Colonel Michaels on the phone to join us. He’ll be happy to know that he has been promoted to Brigadier General in his absence.”

The joyous discussion turned pensive as the team’s lead scientist, Dr. Carlisle, rushed up to the general in alarm: “General, ma’am, excuse me. Something is wrong. The safe room is very hot. In fact, it is too hot to open at this time. And there is no one in the compound. And what is more ominous is this short one-page letter that was left prominently on the counter outside the safe room. It seems crazy."

Startled, General Ivanov asked, "Well, what does it say?"

Dr. Carlisle began to read out the letter as Colonel Michaels had written it:

"In accordance with the instructions sent to us by you, we have cremated our bodies so that no virus from the future can return to your time. You will find our ashes in the safe room. A detailed account of our sixteen years has been meticulously logged onto our computers. Do not allow the next Timenell 2 mission to proceed without taking further precautions. And, if it is sent forward, please equip them with the added provisions we have itemized for the people we left behind.

Refer to the commander's computer log for details."

Colonel Kaddour was stunned and asked, "What do you think it means, General? We had no way of sending them instructions."

Dr. Carlisle went on, "We are in the process of reviewing the commander's log right now to ascertain what Colonel Michaels meant. What our team has relayed to me so far is that we somehow got word to them that they would be bringing back a pathogen to our time – a disease that, they say, would have wiped out all of humanity. It claims they were instructed by you to cremate themselves, explaining that if they came back alive, or if any actual tissue or bone were allowed to return intact, the killer illness would be brought back with them, a plague that would be unstoppable."

General Ivanov was temporarily speechless. Pausing for a moment, she finally said, “I don’t understand this. Please read the complete document and whatever else these people left behind and get back to me. Also, let me know what was meant by ‘the people we left behind.’ Did they find people? I have to make a call.”

It had been prearranged that the President of the United States, and the Prime Ministers of Russia, India, and the People’s Republic of China were to join General Ivanov on a 5-way telephone call scheduled to be broadcast around the world. News agencies across the globe were waiting anxiously to get the word of the return of the *Timenell* crew.

“Am I to tell them that they are all dead? That they killed themselves following my instructions?” the General uttered rhetorically. “Preposterous! I can’t tell them that without knowing what the hell I am talking about. Inform them that the call is being delayed. I’ll be in my office.”

General Ivanov and Colonel Kaddour rushed to the general’s officc and sat down to discuss the situation. Colonel Kaddour spoke first. “Do you think there is anything to this note? Maybe time travel made these people insane. Maybe they discovered some people in the future, and the future-people concocted this ruse to prevent us from sending others into the future after them.”

“I don’t know,” replied the general, shaking her head. “Have your people speed-read those logs and get back to me. One way or another, we must call the other time-probe people and tell them to cancel the upcoming mission. We can’t go ahead with **Timenell 2** now, considering how we lost the entire crew of the first mission. It would be too dangerous to send them forward before we have this all figured out!"

"Scrap the mission?" exclaimed Colonel Kaddour in a shocked voice. "That's pretty extreme. A trillion dollars has been spent preparing for the next mission. If you stop it, you'll be standing at attention in the White House getting your ass chewed, and you'll get the same treatment in the Kremlin. Besides, I know General Warner over at Fort Stewart; he has been anxiously awaiting this send-off for a couple of years. It's the biggest thing to ever happen to him in his career."

"Don't be a fool! General Warner is not an idiot," General Ivanov snapped back. "These people were my friends. And they all died or were killed. Or they killed themselves. We don't know what happened. All I know is that we can't send more people into the future until we determine what went on. And we have a little over 24 hours to figure it out. Get General David Warner on the phone. He's the commander of Fort Stewart and the man in charge of the *Timenell 2* mission."

Suddenly, there was a knock at the office door and Dr. Carlisle walked in. "I have some more disturbing news, General. A team of electricians working about fifty meters beyond the main area said they were just wiring up the new conference room when suddenly, this mass of deteriorating clothing appeared. Mixed within the clothing was what appears to be human remains, some bits of flesh and a lot of bones."

General Ivanov asked, "What do you make of it, doctor?"

Dr. Carlisle replied, "Around the neck of the skeleton were Nicholas Popov's dog tags. He was part of the original crew. I've sent what is left of his remains to be autopsied."

General Ivanov, obviously perturbed, said, "Shouldn't we have left them exactly where they were? In the exact spot, I mean, so that we might better try to figure out what happened?"

Dr. Carlisle nodded in agreement but explained, "The electricians were so startled by the sudden materialization of the remains that they began handling them and examining them to figure out just what they were. Remember, General, these workers were electricians who knew very little about this mission. For these remains to have just appeared out of thin air must have shocked them."

General Ivanov leaned forward. "Where are these electricians now?"

"They were pretty shaken up," Dr. Carlisle replied, somewhat nervously. "A couple of them left the building and went home early. It was way too much for them to handle."

The general was in no mood for additional complications, and spoke in a commanding tone: "Well, get their asses back here right now. They need to be told not to say anything of this to anyone. And we need to decontaminate them. If something did come back from the future, we don't want them spreading it to anyone. That's an order! Get 'em back."

"Excuse me General," Colonel Kaddour interrupted. "I just spoke to General Warner on the phone. As you know, a powerful hurricane is scheduled to hit the coast only a few miles from the *Timenell 2's* takeoff point. He said that high winds were already causing minor power fluctuations at his facility, and that as soon as he received word that the *Timenell* compound had come back, he ordered the *Timenell 2* crew to be sent forward. I'm afraid the next mission is already on its way. They have already left."

Colonel Kaddour's gaze shifted to General Ivanov, "What are you going to tell the world, general?"

Shaking her head, and mumbling under her breath, she replied: "I'm going to tell them to pray."

Chapter 29

Where the Past Becomes the Future

What began as an act of sabotage designed to ruin the *Timenell* mission turned out to be exactly what was needed to ensure the perpetuation of humanity.

Liam was growing old now and he anticipated passing the leadership of the group to his eldest son, a boy born to him and Kristina. Their children were numerous and healthy, as were the children of Stephen and Shari.

The grandchildren of both couples were many with some now producing children of their own. What made up all of humanity ritualistically gathered around the sacred sliding stone every fall.

Liam began to speak, "We are here at the holy place. I stand before our people and repeat the divine things that have been told to me and that I have learned. This is the sacred stone where the ancestors who came from far away gathered to teach us how to live. They knew the secrets of the universe. We have come to promise once again to pass on all these things to our young people, just as they were taught to us. The ancestors were very powerful, and they were real."

Then, the first child of Stephen and Shari, the group's shaman and storyteller, continued, "All the secrets of the Gods have been passed down to us. I will tell you of the stories I have memorized. Our ancestors were giants, very tall. They brought fire to the people and taught us how to hunt, make pottery, and how to plant. They told us of the foods that were good to eat, and of the foods we are not allowed to eat. Of how my own father had drowned and was pulled from the water dead, and that he had life breathed into him again by one of the ancestors. Many witnessed it and were amazed."

Stephen and Shari's youngest daughter spoke up as if on cue and repeated in a chant: "They brought us knowledge of weaving and building and how to care for animals and the little ones."

Then the first grandchild stood and spoke up, "They showed us how we must clasp our hands together and look to the sky for their help, and they will hear us."

Each grandchild was anxious to participate in the ceremony, repeating what their parents had taught them to say. Another child stood up with enthusiasm, "May the Gods come to us once again, and help guide us."

Finally, a young one made everyone proud by speaking with the authority of an adult, saying: "And they told us that we must never forget that they love us and that they will see us and hear us; and to speak to them, all we need do is look to the sky, clasp our hands together, and repeat the sacred word, "Omm!"

These grandchildren would eventually grow up and have children of their own - with every generation afterward trying hard to maintain the rituals begun by the first. All would return to the sliding stone year after year, to swear sacred oaths and to ask for guidance and protection from above.

The End

OUR HUMAN HERDS
Morality doesn't get us into Heaven, morality keeps life on earth from becoming Hell
PHILOSOPHER, S.M. FRITZ
AUTHOR OF THE BOOK, OUR HUMAN HERDS

Philosopher Stephen Martin Fritz has also written a book introducing a new conceptual model of human moral understanding called Dual Morality. He proposes that within each of us evolved two distinct patterns of moral behavior.

These patterns emerged as survival mechanisms to guide our actions in ways appropriate to the circumstances we face at a given time – circumstances of safety and plenty, or circumstances of danger and scarcity. These outlooks make themselves known in their most obvious form: the liberal or conservative ways we feel and act.

When we imagine resources are plentiful, our moral outlook leans liberal and we imagine that most problems can be solved by the proper distribution of plentiful resources. People are poor, only because others are too rich.

In times of struggle and want, our moral outlook leans conservative and we must prioritize people and things.

We are liberal when we can be, conservative when we must be.

Liberalism and conservatism are mistakenly viewed as purely political expressions when, upon reflection, they reveal fundamental, biologically based moral outlooks that we apply to all situations. We are conservative or liberal parents, conservative or liberal employers, conservative or liberal spenders, and even conservative or liberal drinkers.

Through Dual Morality we can better explain the difference between a person's "personality" and their "character," of the differences between "pleasure" and "happiness," and how we can conclude that right is right, wrong is wrong, and how right can also be wrong.

Find out more at www.ourhumanherds.com

www.ingramcontent.com/pod-product-compliance
Ingram Content Group UK Ltd.
Pitfield, Milton Keynes, MK11 3LW, UK
UKHW022031170625
6447UKWH00007B/724

9 798344 792767